THE LIGHT WAS BRIGHTER

MANISH CHATURVEDI

Made with ♥ on the Notion Press Platform
www.notionpress.com

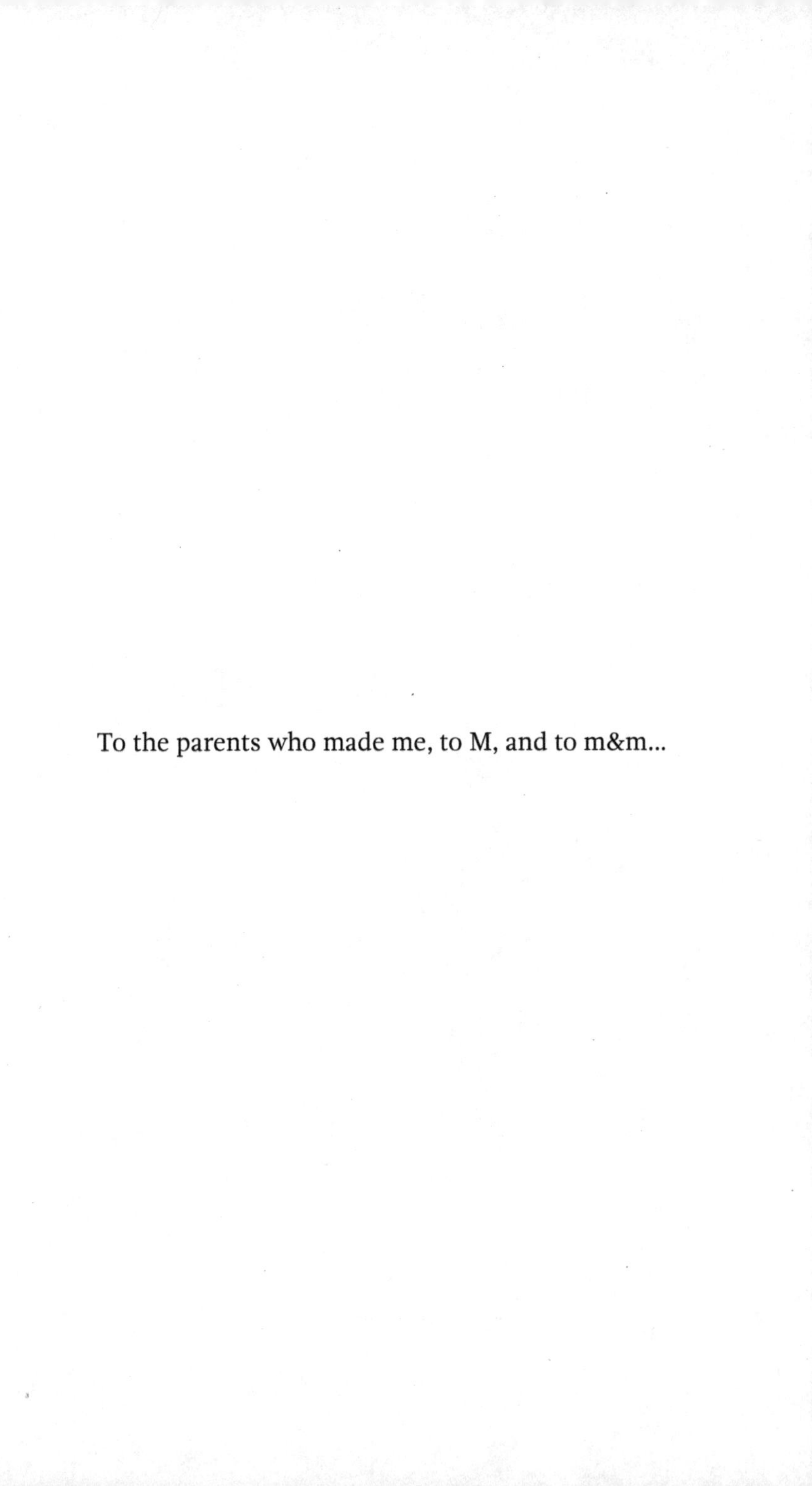

To the parents who made me, to M, and to m&m...

Contents

Disclaimer

This is a work of fiction. All names, characters, organizations, locations, events and incidents in this book are either the product of the author's imagination or used in a fictitious manner. Any resemblance to actual persons, living or dead, or actual events is purely coincidental.

PART 1: A diary is found

In the middle of March 2016, large-scale digging started on a piece of land just east of the IT College in Lucknow. A necessary evil, perhaps, to allow a new college building to come up. Scores of mango trees were uprooted; some, mercifully, to be transplanted on the botanical institute grounds. During the clearing up, a low wall - clearly old, but of indefinite vintage - was unceremoniously broken down. Ramesh, a contract worker driving the JCB digger, found a bundle of papers inside a plastic bag, partially damaged by the rubble, but still readable. There were hand-written pages in English – a language which Ramesh could read, and understand, as long as it was simple – and he recognized some of the names there, so decided to take it away to show his ex-employer.

Chapters 1 to 5 are entries from this diary.

CHAPTER I

20/11/15 - 21/11/15

[Friday, 20/11/2015, 9PM]

'Arjun, I have a deal for you.' The old man was watching me intently, and the words tried to register in my brain. This was a strange turn the day was taking, I thought.

But let me start at the beginning.

Today morning, when I was getting ready to go to office, I was in a more-than-usual "thoughtful" mode. And after much grinding of the wheels, was about to decide that some kind of closure had been reached, as far as my affairs were concerned.

Even the deepest pain goes away, finally. You, basically, learn to get over disappointments. Provided you give it time and take your medicines regularly. Anjali went out of my life in October – on a shitty date I have been actively trying to forget, and so will not name. After a few weeks of feeling unwanted, the questioning, confusion and self-recrimination had changed from a hammering-between-the-ears to a memory-of-an-ache-somewhere. I convinced myself to get over what I had taken as a defeat (if not a disaster) and resolved to try and find new meaning out of it. And if you really think about it: though rejection is extremely painful, it leaves your conscience clear. At least YOU were not the one to ditch a commitment!

Raju's presence helped, because he was Anjali's cousin after all. So much so, that coming to my office one afternoon, he said that we should forgive and forget. I had nothing to forgive him for, and though I could not forget what I went through with Anjali, I was now ready to forget

Raju's behavior after that fateful day in my life. Anyway, hands were shook, backs were slapped, and our friendship renewed so quickly that we sat down with beer and kababs that Saturday itself. On this ongoing journey to regain normality, I also tried to socialize, to the extent of attending a Kayastha-sabha meeting. A community gathering whose main purpose appeared to be eating, and for scanning prospective matches for boys and girls. I tried to keep myself busy, in other words, in more conventional ways. Less than two weeks ago, I had gone home to Allahabad for Diwali. From the noise & smoke of fireworks and *puja*, along with familiar sweets, I tried to rebuild normalcy. I was still fending off questions from the parents about marriage plans, etc., but I think I returned to Lucknow with my mental life a little more stable. Till today, that is, because Colonel Rana happened to me today.

Admittedly, Colonel Ranveer Rana had actually "happened" to me earlier this year, in February, when I had first rented this room from him. What I am writing about though is my strange encounter with him a few hours ago.

Ok, so I live in this room which is an extension of the Retired Colonel Rana's bungalow in Nirala Nagar, near the old post office. My current rental agreement still has about two months to go, and I was hoping to extend it. Provided he agreed to that, of course. The rent is reasonable, my office conveniently nearby, I have gotten used to the neighborhood, and for help, there is Kishan, the gardener who, while taking care of Colonel's garden, occasionally does odd-jobs for me as well.

Anyway, today, i.e. the third Friday of November, on my way back from office, I walked the last 15 minutes after getting down at the turn from the University road, and entered the main gate of the house, braced after the walk. It is kind of ironic that I was thinking about my future right then – turning over the various potentialities, playing with them like a kitten fiddles with a ball of string – and I was actually feeling good enough that my thoughts were without the morbidity of even a few days ago. As I walked to the side of the house I turned my head to look towards the main door. Kishan was standing there, arranging a plastic bag on to the handle of his bicycle. Let us do it now, I thought, and turned away from the stairs leading to my room on the first floor. Walking towards Kishan, I noticed that he was looking different. And then I realized - he was wearing clean pants and shirt and appeared more self-confident than usual. As I approached, he got his bicycle off the stand, and turned it around towards the gate. His dark, pondering face was on me as he raised his hand in a practiced, more-friendly-than-subservient salute. I acknowledged him and asked if Colonel Rana is at home.

'Where will he go? Sitting on his favorite "rest-chair" and reading something all the time! You want to meet him.' The last was not a question, but I answered, anyway.

'Yes. Everything going well with you, Kishan?'

'All is well. The one-with-the-blue-umbrella is still there.' He gestured with his forefinger sky-ward.

'Absolutely.' I replied in Hindi, and went towards the main door. I have to admit that his comment raised my spirits further. Though there is really nothing significant to look forward to in life (yes, yes, we know why, right?), there is some solace to be found in relying on an all-encompassing presence. Infantile, maybe, but it felt good then.

Kishan placed his bicycle on the side stand and came with me. Pushing the main door ajar, he shouted with his mouth near the opening, aimed at the unseen Colonel - '...your tenant has come to meet!'

I opened the door farther to go inside, and Kishan turned around and went his way. I had no idea what I was getting into, of course. We rarely do, beforehand. It was only later that I started wondering that if I had not come to meet the colonel that evening, I may not have gotten into this mess. Well, one can wonder all one wants, it does not cost anything.

The door opened into a green-walled passage, and the marble floor looked so clean that I felt compelled to wipe my shoes vigorously on the doormat. After a thorough wiping, I stepped inside finally and headed to the drawing room towards the back of the house, passing the cluttered kitchen to the left, and a closed door to the right. I called out his name tentatively, and hearing a cough, followed it inside.

The drawing room faced a garden towards the back, and there was some light still peeping in. More like twilight, actually, and the room was in shadows. I could not make out clearly, but he was sitting in an armchair towards the back of the room, facing inside. Should I turn on a light, I asked him, but he gestured that question away.

'Come in, come in, son. Sit here.'

'Good evening. How are you, Sir?'

'I'm like a creaking and rusted old tank. How else will I be?'

Though I could not make out his face, the voice did not appear to have any bitterness in it. That came later, but right then he appeared in a cheerful mood. Anyway, I sat down next to him on a straight chair, and smiling back at him, rubbed my hands together – more in nervousness than anticipation. He looked quite old and run-down, in fact older than I had ever seen him. Average height, thin but well-combed grey hair, a ragged moustache, weak chin, with the jowls getting heavier. The eyes behind the glasses were active and curious. I must have been sitting down with him after many months – don't even remember when the last time was. Anyway, I tried to be polite.

'Shall I get you something? Water, or...'

'Get out of here - you are my guest! But.... that chap will come in around 7, so.... Okay, how about you fix me a drink? And one for yourself, of course.' And after a pause, 'do your parents know you drink?'

I was not sure how to answer that last question, and only laughed back as I got up to fix his whisky and soda, following instructions and getting everything from the bar and the small fridge underneath. I handed it over, and then poured myself one from the same bottle of Teacher's, adding some water to it.

'To your health, son.' He sipped a greedy sip, and then added - 'I cannot bloody well toast *my* own health, anyway!' He did not miss my grimace at that. 'But let me not worry you about my health. Tell me, how are you? Liking your room, I hope, and no complaints?'

'No, no, everything is fine. Only wanted to talk to you about extending the agreement further. You know that it expires at the end of December, right?'

'No problem, we'll do that!' He was dismissive again, and I got the feeling that he was weighing heavier matters on his mind. 'I have also not heard any complaints about you.' His smile was more scary than friendly, and my sixth sense woke up again - our Colonel Rana is not all-there. Some screw has come loose, perhaps. But I have to make the right noises and show the right expressions. At least till he does not actually starts behaving crazily, ha, ha.

'Thank you! Please let me know when we can sign the new agreement, and I will come.'

'I will ask Yadav to take care of it..., uhhhh.' He had forgotten my name, of course. I told him, but he fell silent after repeating it once, staring at his half-empty glass now. Perhaps he was reconsidering his statement about there being "no problem." I fidgeted and tried to drink my whisky quietly. My insides started getting warmed soon, and I tried to relax, but felt I had to keep my attention focused on him – who knows where his conversation would veer next. He stayed quiet for a few minutes. My unease increased, as we sipped, and the day gathered darkness outside and turned into night. He gestured at the light switch, and I took his cue to turn on the pedestal lamp. I could see him better now, and it was not a pleasant sight.

'I will take your leave?' and I took the last sip of my drink.

'Nonsense! Sit for some more time. Here, make me another drink.'

I did not mind the whisky, actually. And it was marginally better sitting here, rather than in my hermit-like room. If only we could get something to nibble with it... Then I noticed him staring at me, and his mouth opened.

'Arjun, I want to propose a deal to you.' He was watching me intently, and the words tried to register in my brain.

(You see now how strange a turn the day was taking? But this was just the beginning.)

'Deal? Seriously?' I tried to smile, which slipped away under his intense gaze, though I managed to lock my eyes with those (perhaps crazy?) eyes.

'Yes, a deal. You do something for me, and I will give something in return – that kind of "deal"! Are you interested in hearing about the mission?' He kept staring.

'...Okay', I said and took another sip, while trying to imagine what chore he was going to ask me to do. Mission? Really?

'Fine, son! But I also want your promise that what I am about to tell you stays between the two of us – whether we agree to the deal or not. Do I have that? Good, now... first things first – you must be thinking if I am asking you to do something illegal, right?' And he smiled again. It was ghastly!

'*Arrey* no, Colonel Sahib, I would never have to worry about that with you!' I really had not gone that far in my thinking. But he waved his free hand impatiently.

'That is kind of you, but I assure you, it will be wilder than a robbery! Ok, the deal is this – you have to go and stay somewhere for.... let's say about six months, and do something for me, and in exchange I will pass on half of my assets to you. That's it!' He waited for that to sink in, and then seemed to remember something else. 'There is another thing. You will really be gone for only a few minutes!'

He sat back and drained his glass, his eyes wandering around the room, and finally settling on a wall poster somewhere behind my back. I turned to follow his gaze and could only see a blown-up image of white pebbles, smoothened by running water. I turned back slowly and checked my glass. What did he mean by that – was it a few months or a few minutes? Of course, he has had too much to drink and is probably babbling. But he appeared sober otherwise, so... the only conclusion is that the old man has gone crazy. But he was not finished.

'My assets add up to more than 3 Crores. Mostly property, but some jewelry, stocks and a bit of cash. I have to leave something for relatives and charity, but even with half of that you will be pretty well off, I believe. What do you say, son? I know you must be thinking that I have gone cuckoo. But bear with me, and when I explain all, you will know.'

I must have blinked, because he paused for effect. I was still speechless - imagining how much is 1.5 Crore rupees - when he spoke again, his voice lower now.

'Now, listen closely!' He was not smiling at all. 'There is an old mango grove next to the IT College. It is called Chand Bagh. I think it was constructed by one of the rulers of Awadh – perhaps Bahadur Shah himself, or maybe someone even earlier. It does not really matter who! In this garden, there is a small entrance...' He paused again, and I realized I was holding my breath – 'this entrance or gate takes you to the year 1966.' He stopped to see my reaction.

I got up, my head feeling heavy, 'it is late, sir. I think I should go.' He looked at me without raising his head, only his eyeballs moving under those bushy-white eyebrows. I hesitated. Was it wise to leave him alone in this condition? I saw that my glass still had a little whisky left in it. I ventured, 'hope you are feeling ok', and picked up my glass to empty it. He shook his head – 'no, I am not. But that is beside the point right now!'

You don't believe me, and any sane person would not! Hell, I did not believe it myself when my son first told me about it. Sanju, poor boy....' With the back of his hand, he wiped his eyes angrily, and with a visible effort controlled himself.

'Fine. I expected this. And so, you will have to do a recce. Go on a short visit, controlled and timed – and then you come back and tell me if you still do not believe me. Okay?'

I was shaking my head now, still standing, and trying to understand what I was getting into. Where was he sending me? Perhaps there was no harm to indulging him on this reconnaissance trip. But first the big question – why!

'Ok, Colonel Saheb – I am still not saying yes, and that is because I still do not see what is it that you want me to do. Please understand.' I was requesting to his saner self – it must be there somewhere. And he actually appeared sober and serious now, his teeth clenched tightly.

'I understand, dammit! What I am asking you to do (he was chewing each word and spitting it out now) is to go and see for yourself that there is a bloody portal to the past a few kilometers from here! And every time you enter this, it takes you back to the same day and time – about 1530 hours on the afternoon of 9th November 1966. And once you have seen it and believe me, then your real mission would start. And this mission, this job, is to prevent an accident from happening. That's it! You complete this job, and you will get half of my property – all legal and clear – and no questions asked!'

He stopped to take a deep breath, exhaled, and realized that he was still holding his whisky glass in his hand. He placed it on the side table, with a thick clunk of glass against wood, and looked up. I was scared from inside now, but also curious. Finally, I heard myself whisper – 'why?'

'Why!? Isn't that obvious, son? I am trying to undo a bloody accident that happened many years ago! This accident, this unplanned event was my mistake..., someone died, and, that consumed my entire life. My marriage, my personal life, my next generation – everything! And when this, this... GATE, miraculously opened in front of me, would I hesitate to take this chance? The chance to go back and stop the mess from even happening? You tell me now –

am I wrong to think that?'

I did not know what to say and could only nod a hesitant head. At first, but then quickly turned that into a shake as I realized his question. My mind was still reeling, trying to grapple with the idea of a time-travel portal just off Faizabad Road.

'How is this possible? And how did you discover it?' And the even more personal question – 'why me, Colonel Saheb?'

He appeared very old and very tired by now. 'I really don't know how this is possible, but it is real! I have been there, and back, and I will tell you all I know about it, but not today. I can answer your last question now, though. But..., could you give me some water to drink?'

His sudden change of topic left me disoriented for a second, but I gathered myself and poured him the water. Then I filled my own glass with some water and gulped it quickly.

'After my wife passed away, and then my son... all my relatives started avoiding me, and even my friends became distant. Understandably so, I guess. So, there was really no one else I could recruit for this mission so far. Except myself, of course.'

He paused again, and I waited him out. He is old and not in the best of health, obviously. But still...

'I really tried myself – went there three times, made notes, maps, collected the necessary information I would need, etcetera. When I came down with fever last week, I decided that as soon as I recover, I will go and finish the job this time. But I have still not recovered, and on top of that the doctor tells me that I have perhaps only a few days left to live. Unless I am connected to a ventilator. Which I have refused!'

His eyes were shining again, and this contrast between his words and the appearance hit me hard. I am sure my face had a what-the-fuck expression on it, and I could only stare at him.

'So, you see, son? Your coming here today was a clear case of "God moving in mysterious ways his wonders to perform". Don't you see the beautiful logic? It is perfect – a truly win-win situation!'

'But, but... you don't look... sick, at all!' I was fumbling for expression, and for once it was nothing to be ashamed of. The news was mind-numbing, but some "nobler" feelings were intruding now – of being in the right place, of being useful, and of making something out of this for myself.

'Come now, son. We are way beyond niceties at this late stage.' He actually smiled, and I felt tears squeezing out of the corner of my eyes. Wiping them away brusquely, I realized that my mind was made up – at least for the first trip.

'Ok sir! I think I will go for this trial. Let us talk about the main mission – and our deal – only after that. Hope it is ok?'

'Thank you, Arjun. I appreciate your understanding! And now I will get some rest. Let us meet tomorrow morning here again. Come as early as you can get ready. Good night.'

I dragged my feet away, my mind still caught in the impossible imagery of the old Colonel Rana – a man trying to fight the past, falling sick and about to die!! As I turned around to look at him once more, he had picked up his phone and was trying to call someone. 'Good night', I mumbled and went out.

When I came out, a man was alighting from his scooter and parking it. The lawyer, or the accountant, or someone else. Does he know that he is soon going to lose a client? Anyway, it was dark now, and we passed each other by, quietly.

Tomorrow.

• • •

[Saturday, 21/11/2015, 1:30PM]

This is what Colonel Rana told me today morning –

'So, you understand the plan? Go through that bloody gate, look for the water tank towards north-east, get out quickly to the side-street, head to Faizabad Road, and then observe what is happening there! A man and a woman arguing - she on a rickshaw, he on the ground - and then everyone disperses. You turn around and come back the way you had gone. I have given you some other details, but beyond that, I have no strength left to give, nor do I particularly want to. This briefcase with all the papers, currency, and some other goodies, will be yours after this recce – unless you come back and say you don't want to go ahead. For whatever reason. And finally, here are some coins for you to keep, just as a contingency.

I will emphasize again - the boy you will see is the main cog of this whole wheel you are going to climb on and ride. You will have to make friends with him, and I have a plan for that as well. But that comes later.

Arjun, thanks for going on this, this.... I don't know what to call it! Pilgrimage, Mission, perhaps even a Folly? But an Adventure, most certainly.'

His eyes had started shining again as he explained, and behind the sickly pallor that was even more visible in the daylight, it seemed to me that he would really have preferred to go back and do it himself. It is only now, after turning it over in my mind some more that I have started noticing possible dilemmas, incongruities – if he goes himself. But then I realize that perhaps he knows it, and never would have done it himself, anyway! It would cause too many impossibilities.

And what about my visit? What am I getting into? My first time-traveling trip coming up in less than two hours...

CHAPTER II

21/11/15

[Saturday, 21/11/2015, 9:45PM]

It was an old wall, low, broken down in parts, and constructed from thin reddish bricks you may still see in many old buildings across north India. The wall ended just a few feet after the curved opening in it, and that could be why human passage may have been rare through it. Assuming it was rare, that is. I noticed another thing. The opening was beautifully shaped with an arch at the top, but was obviously made for dwarfs, with only four feet between the ground and the tip of the arch. Being inside an enclosed orchard, in the middle of scattered mango trees and a general air of abandonment, it was surely unfrequented. Though I do not think of myself as the most observant person around, the fact is I had never even thought about this place before, let alone going inside, while living nearby for a few years now. I mean, I must have passed by in front of it many times before. Admittedly, never on foot, as far as I can remember, but still. I do most of my walking to and from the office – provided the weather is ok – but rarely for leisure otherwise!

So..., I crouched down by the side of this little opening in the wall, and balancing myself with a palm against it, tried to observe it better. Thankfully, no spider-webs that I could see. There were traffic noises from not too far away, but the air was still around me. Then I felt a slight vibration in the wall under my palm. '...shit!' I cursed under my breath, realizing that I had to do it quickly if I did not want to lose my nerve and walk back – untouched and ignorant.

'Go!' I exhorted myself and moved forward in a duck walk, still crouching. My right knee, and then my head went under the wall and came up against some resistance – like a strong soap-bubble film or a stronger-than-usual spider web – though I could see nothing. And only because I knew and expected it, I went ahead and pushed (perhaps even physically), the invisible film parted, and I passed through to the other side.

Straightening, I realized that I had stepped into someplace else, and no amount of preparation by dear old Colonel Ranveer Singh Rana could have readied me for the experience itself. It was disorienting – I was in a wild forest growing, and glowing brightly, in afternoon sunlight. On the other side, from where I had come, the wall had been part of an abandoned ruin, and there had been a few mango trees spread around. But that was on that side. I swayed a little and realized that the air itself had changed. There was a smell – reminiscent of raw greenness and life – and I could only wonder at how strong it was.

You are still alive, you bastard - I told myself, and drawing a deep breath, looked around. It was certainly wild – the trees were growing unconstrained by fences, wires or axes – but still managed to appear like a garden. If Colonel Rana was right, it was November here too, but it certainly felt cooler on this side of the wall. Or, was I just imagining it? And it was very quiet. No audible traffic noises from the Faizabad road that should (still) be only a few meters away. So, this is how it was about half a century ago, on a November afternoon in the year 1966?! I shook my head to clear the cobwebs on my mind and tried to remember the Colonel's instructions.

First, check yourself, and make sure you have no visible signs of the 21st century on you. Leather sandals, my flat-fronted khaki pants with a plain white shirt, unshaven (holiday today), along with some coins the Colonel had generously handed me; just in case I decide to be adventurous and start shopping on this side. Patting my pockets, I felt my keys, which I had kept with me anyway, and then cursed aloud, as my hand touched something hard and rectangular. I had brought along my new iPhone, which had turned itself off – as I noticed. The pressures of time travel, I mused; worrying slightly about my big consolation purchase after Anjali's departure from my life. Oh well, I only have to make sure it stays in my pocket while I am here. And stop thinking about her, will you?!

Second, look for a water-tank, northeast of where you come out of the gate. Gate? I glanced back at the inconsequential-looking opening - this damn thing is a time-portal! I raised my head, searched around and saw the brick & concrete tank; a plain but obviously new construction, peeking over the trees, and announcing its whitewashed manmade-ness. There would be a gate under that water-tank that leads out to a side road. I had to turn right on that road, walk a few steps to the Faizabad road, turn left and observe something about to happen; or already started.

Okay, let us go. And though my mind was reeling and my stomach queasy, now that I had come this far, I found that it was not difficult to will my feet to start moving. It was nice to walk through these trees – no debris of human packaging here (now); no plastic bags or shiny paper wrappers or broken beer bottles. And there were birds! As I brushed against a low shrub, a panic of sparrows, speckled brown & white, appeared, flying out in the opposite direction, and then slowly settled down inside another nearby shrub. It felt like a dream, where unheard of things happen. And it WAS a dream, really – how else could I explain my presence here almost fifty years ago?

As I neared the base of the water-tank, I could hear a bell, ringing rhythmically, and thought, somewhat absurdly, of this as a warning signal. There was a clearing in front of me now; and I could see a charpoy and an old bamboo-knit stool next to a small brick construction – about the size of a room. There was a rope tied across the clearing, with a bright pink-white thin cloth towel spread on it. For a moment, I panicked - humanity! There was no one in sight, but I knew (had been told) there was a man inside that brick shelter, behind the thin cloth curtain hanging in front of the opening. I had no business with this person, as per my instructions, and pushing down the feeling of dread, I moved on. To the opening in the hedge that ran across the boundary of this whole forest-cum-garden. This gate was put together by sticks, and instead of being hinged, was tied by jute twines to the hedge on one side. I moved the makeshift structure away gingerly and stepping out, pushed it close behind me. There was a dip in the ground, and then it rose up again to meet the road. I looked around. The absence of trash was still glaringly obvious, and required mental adjustments of various kinds. I breathed deeply and climbed on to the road.

A few feet away to my left, there was a bullock-cart going down the road, the gentle sound of its bell receding as it moved away. There were two men sitting in the cart, their backs towards me, and in any case, they had no role to play in this drama - as far I knew. So, I turned and started walking down the street towards the main road. My feet moved easily over the narrow, tarred surface, till I came to a steaming pile of dung, and walked around it. Colonel Rana missed telling me about this one, I thought, and then tried to remember what next: a cyclist would be coming from behind me any time now and will overtake me. I resisted the urge to turn around.

Suddenly, a dark, pinched face was leaning towards me, staring unabashedly, as he cycled by. A young, thin body draped with a loose pair of pants (gray), a cotton shirt (white), and shining hair (oiled!) over a hungry face. The bicycle looked very basic but functional, and there was a cloth bag swinging happily from the handle. I looked up at him and then turned my gaze, as naturally as I could, down towards the road. Not looking for conversation or confrontation. As instructed. He cycled on, weaving a little – the road was his for the moment – and then slowed down as he neared the junction ahead of us and turned right on the main road. Even though it seemed that the bicycle had appeared sooner than I thought, I could not but marvel how it was all going according to the program given to me by the Colonel. I had to turn left on this road, so would have nothing further to do with this person. I kept telling myself that, consolingly.

As I neared the junction, more traffic could now be seen and heard: An Ambassador car – big, black, but not really shiny, some pedestrians, a group of cyclists, and an occasional scooter; all these passed by on Faizabad road, going about their respective businesses. A few minutes ago (actually, many years in future!!), this very road had been full of traffic - cars, motorcycles, tempos, even small trucks, etc. If I turned right and walked down a little distance, I should see the place where I had entered the garden next to the IT College. I shook my head and forced myself back to the present (past!?). From what I could see so far, the clothes were mostly dull colors - blacks, whites, and browns - except for some brightly colored sarees or *dupattas* that stood out. I slowed down, as if considering my options, and then turned left at the junction. At this corner was the big banyan tree, its trunk circled by red, yellow and saffron-colored threads, and looking much greener than I had seen it in the present. A makeshift wooden stall was leaning under this fully-grown but still young tree: a vessel over an earthen oven next to it, a clay pot of drinking water sitting nearby, and a man standing off to one side, looking intently at something happening on the road.

Right on time! This is what I had come to see; to finally confirm if the Colonel's tale was just that, or something as real as the warmth of the sun and the hardness of the ground I could feel. I was standing in the afternoon sunlight of a day on this road, more than two decades before I was born; and I was part of the scene – it was not a movie! And the scene that was unfolding in front of me? My eyes caught sight of her then – in a pink and white *salwar*-suit, with dark hair held back by a band. The *kurta* was tight enough to hug her, and she sat straight. Similar in some ways to the heroines I had seen in old Hindi movies, though leaner than those well-fed screen goddesses. And even from that distance, I could clearly make out the intensity in her face – mixed with some anger right then. Or, maybe the sunlight was just brighter around us here?

A cycle rickshaw was stopped on the other side of the road, the girl was perched on the seat and talking to a young man who was standing (awkwardly, it seemed, because he kept shifting his weight) on the ground. The rickshaw-wala was standing next to them, holding the handle, waiting patiently for the conversation to get over. Behind them, there were only trees, as far as I could see. As the conversation progressed, her face toughened further - as if she was not liking the situation at all, perhaps even regretting getting into it. During the few seconds of their conversation that I was witness to, even though she visibly relaxed towards the end, the toughness never really left her face. Perhaps this was the reason I did not particularly like her when seeing her for the first time (on that November afternoon in the year 1966).

For someone from the 21st century, it was not an unusual scene - a girl and a boy together on the side of a road, except for the traffic nuisance it was likely to create - but it was obviously something of a novelty in these times. Besides the stall-keeper, there were a few other passers-by – on both sides of the road – who had slowed down and were looking on with frank curiosity, as if at some accident!

The "*chai-wala*" was dark, with *khichdi* hair, loose pajamas around his waist, a long white-gone-to-brown *kurta*, and a black *Sherwani-type* coat – looking like a filmi, down-on-his-luck Urdu poet. As he turned towards me to welcome a customer, the unbuttoned jacket flapped open, and I got the impression of a large crow with carelessly raised wings. His feet were covered with army-issue canvas shoes, with the right one torn at the big-toe. He smiled, the cratered face (chicken-pox?) crinkled, and his teeth came into view – surprisingly clean! I smiled back in a reflex action. He spoke in an unfamiliar though understandable dialect of *Hindi* – 'what will you have, *bhaiya ji*?' Being nervous, I overcompensated by trying to be too smart, though keeping my voice normal – 'what **do** you have?' and smiled to convey the humor. He folded his hands, bent his head and started shaking it gently. 'What will this *gareeb* afford to have, *sahib*?' But he was also smiling, and I realized that we were playing out some kind of a social ritual. I immediately liked this guy, but when I responded by folding my own hands and laughed out, he must have been taken by surprise. My laughter sounded obscenely loud in that still afternoon (there were practically no traffic noises, especially no horns!) Even the couple on the road stopped their conversation and looked at us. I felt uneasy and unsure under the gazes from around me, and to hide my confusion, turned around and requested my new friend for 'chai'. He had just recently recovered from my laughter, when my mode of request hit him gently. He bore this too with fortitude. 'I will prepare it fresh right now!' and as he started bustling around in preparation, I turned around again to observe the road. The rickshaw-wala was now climbing on his seat, and Mr. X had moved sideways, almost off the road, with hands held out in placation. The pink & white lady was gathering herself, with one hand now holding a bar on the side, and the other pressing down a green bag (books and what else?) in her lap. As the wheels started moving, she turned to look up again, her gaze travelled around slowly and met mine, from across the road. I did not break it, and neither did she – for as long as I could see her face. I felt a wave of irritation creeping on. She was trying to stare me down! And years before I was even born!! I sighed and turned away, as her ricksha moved farther down the road towards IT College.

'Where are you from, *bhaiya ji*? At least not from *Nakhlau*?' He had set up a large vessel on the earthen stove and was fanning the wood fire from the opening on the side, crouched down on the ground. I replied, 'No, no – have come from Banaras!' As soon I said that, I wondered if that came out correctly or not. 'Kashi', he observed shortly – a hint of a query hanging on to the last *ee* of Kashi, but nothing else conveyed that he was correcting – or disbelieving me. 'What's your name, brother?' I asked in Hindi, and he replied briefly – 'I am Ram Aasray.' Then he was glancing behind me, and I turned around to come face to face with Mr. X himself. This was the man I had come for – perhaps the single most important reason why Colonel Rana was making this deal with me. He looked about my age (though I knew he was younger then, than I am in 2015) and was wearing what seemed to be the standard colors of the time - gray pants & white shirt - the shirt was tucked-in and sleeves rolled up above the elbows. He walked around me, without acknowledgement of any kind, and kept going till he reached Ram Aasray, who was crouching next to the oven. Then, peremptorily, 'wash my hands, a little?' His voice was high pitched; above-average height, gangly, with a thin moustache perched on the upper lip, and a thick dark mop of hair on top, close-cropped at the bottom and sides. There were black sandals on his feet, well-maintained, sturdy and clean. And as my newly-made friend straightened up to get water from a pot, Mr. X started humming, still higher pitched than normal – and I could recognize the song - '*...dil jo na keh sakaa, wohi raa-ze-dil keh-ne ki raat aayi...* (what the heart could not convey/ that same inner-secret/ the night has come to share.)' A romantic number by Rafi-sab, with a jazz-like score and a melancholic mood. I mentally thanked this old-timer for reminding me of it. Could not remember which movie it was from, and thought of Googling as soon as I return.

And, just like that – very likely triggered by the thought of internet and videos – I panicked again. What the hell was I doing? I should hurry back to that blasted hole in the wall! As instructed, I should have just returned after observing the scene. But here I was - getting into transactions, both conversational and monetary! Will this change anything, impact anything back in my 2015?! All the time-travel stories I have ever read, drum this caution into the reader repeatedly. But could a tea and some innocuous chatting change anything? On reflection, at that moment, it did not seem possible. And then, another worry hit me: will I even be able to get back to my time? In my nervousness, I took out the coins from my wallet and spread them on my palm. There were three 2-paise coins, gray colored and wavy around the perimeter, two 5-paise coins, same color but a little bigger & square-shaped, and a couple each of 10- and 50-paise coins. Colonel Rana had not told me the price of road-side tea in 1966, so I had no idea what I would have to pay. But social conventions are strong, and can override the novelty, even the panic, of time-traveling. So, I told myself that since I have already asked for tea, and he had already started boiling the stuff, I cannot very well leave now. Hopefully the taste of the tea from 1966 would be worth it! Mr. X had stopped humming his song and was in the process of lighting a cigarette. I turned towards the road, and tried to remember how it looks in my time. There should be the huge expanse of the Reserve Police Lines across the street, but I could only see the trees, and some buildings peeking out to the left – probably where the New Hyderabad colony would be.

'*Chai...*", I heard the voice behind me and turned to take the clay mug. Steam was rising from it, and when I took a tentative sip, found it to be hot, sweet and (a little too-) milky, but the flavor was different and not bad. "How much?" I asked him to get that part out of the way. He only shook his head gently – "leave it *bhaiya.* We are not going to take money from someone who is coming from our Kashi!" So, I sipped the tea and considered my options. First - make the right noises. "*Achcha,* you are also from there! Still, I will not drink just like that." Second – show generosity. I took out the coins with my other hand, and handed him

10-paise, almost forcing him to accept. He took it finally, and folded his palms, his head bowed a little. I bobbed my head in response and offered a compliment – "tea is very good!" "*Meherbaani*", he murmured, and turned away. After my generosity, perhaps he was embarrassed now, and unsure.

But really, the tea was tasting better by the sip; I could also pick a faint whiff of jaggery and enjoyed that, while still looking around. To the left, the road continued, but there was no flyover there yet, so it was completely flat, and I could see far into what I imagined would be the beginnings of Nishatganj. The Indira Bridge is yet to be built, perhaps not till the 70s. I will have to look it up. When I get back.... On my right, I could see the IT College intersection, and the road continuing beyond towards Daliganj and beyond. And it struck me again – there are so few buildings around. Only the IT College on my right, the domes of Lucknow University on the other side of the road, probably extending all the way towards the Monkey Bridge in the distance. No apartment buildings, no shopping complexes. Lots of trees and very few vehicles! Wow – just to imagine what my eyes would see if I walked towards the University and then on to the Gomti river?

I emptied the *kulhad* with a last gulp and tried to snap back to reality; this "reality" of being in a time before my birth! Ram Aasray was asking something – 'are you searching for some place, *bhaiya*?' He had concern on his face, and I noticed that Mr. X was also looking at me now. I smiled bravely, trying to inject some melancholy in my voice, 'nothing, really! Just my address.' And then, without waiting to get his reaction, 'will get going now, *bhai*.' I turned with a raised hand of farewell and started crossing the road. I did this hoping to buy some time, because a thought had come to my mind. I waited, dawdling, till a passing *rickshaw* slowed down, the driver leaning back to slow down, and nodding his head at me, 'should we take you somewhere, *babu saheb*?' It was such a graceful invitation to use his services, that I could not help but smile. 'I don't have to go now, but tell me something. How much will you take for Daliganj?' He stopped, happy to chat, and definitely looking forward to a fare. 'Very little, *saheb*. Where will you go in Daliganj?' I glanced behind him and saw Mr. X leaving the stall. I was going to follow him – that was the bright idea I had had! But he was coming towards me, crossing the road quickly. And then he was next to us, and asking the *rickshaw-wala* himself, 'you will go?' It appeared to me that he was intentionally being rude, or maybe it was just my guilty conscience – the proverbial twig in the thief's beard. The man looked at me questioningly. I clarified hastily, 'go, go...', with a wave of my hand, and started walking away towards the IT college to the right. After a few steps, I turned around slowly and noticed the *rickshaw*, with Mr. X in it of course, moving the other way, towards Nishatganj and other places that may or may not yet exist. So much for my plan, I thought, and then decided to continue walking. I was really curious to see how the IT crossing looked. A few more minutes, and then it would be time to leave this place.

To my left, I could make out the gate of the Police Lines now. Hmmm.., so it was already there in 1966! Too many trees in the front though, for it to be visible from a little distance away. I turned my head to the right and noticed that I was crossing the exact place where I had gone in a few minutes ago, but in the year 2015!! And, this was a really weird idea - what if I went inside and crossed that gate again in the same direction? If the gate is still open in this time, will it take me farther in the past – by another few decades, for example? Or could there be some kind of circularity effect, or....

Suddenly all my thoughts were drawn back to the present as my eyes came upon, and then took in the entrance to the IT College. It was as if Holi was being played over there, and a riot of colors overwhelmed my senses - from about five different shades of bougainvillea flowers blossoming over and around the arch! It was beautiful!! I have – in my admittedly limited experience so far – rarely seen such natural beauty. The gate was facing (as it still does) South, and the rays of the winter afternoon sun were falling at it from the side, at about 45° in the sky, and the colors were lit up audaciously. Behind the flowers, the Roman columns of the College building stood magnificent and proud. I stopped and closed my eyes to capture that scene and realized that I am probably looking at a different sky from what I had been used to, a glimpse of another part of the universe. I felt a subtle pain in my forehead, somewhere between my eyes, as I tried to imagine this vastness.

A song came on my lips, unbidden– "*jeevan se lambe hain, bandhu...*," (longer than a lifespan, friend...) then an associated memory - a movie-scene – of a brown, desolate landscape, stretching away to the horizon, and broken only by contours in the land itself. In the scene, the camera zooms in, and more details could be seen. Not sure which movie or actor, but definitely sung by Manna Dey. A reformed convict walking away from it all – that's what I seem to remember. Lost in this train of thought, my hand sub-consciously dived into my pocket to take out my iPhone, before I realized what I was doing, and snatched my hand away. I should get back to my present!

In front of me were the cross-roads of Faizabad Road and University Road – the "world-famous" IT *Chauraha.* And it was not much to look at now; just a simple, unremarkable intersection of two roads. If I turned right at that intersection and walked for about two km, I would be able to see the place I will live fifty years later. I shivered, hugged myself tight and turned around. That is when I noticed a scooter rider – coming from the Nishatganj side – and he turned his head to stare at me, as I waited to cross the road. He had sunglasses on, and a blue bush-shirt – very dapper! This place keeps surprising me, I told myself. And immediately corrected; it was the "time", not the "place"! Of course, the "surprises" had started because I had done something unplanned, something that Colonel Rana had not experienced, and so had not been able to tell me to expect!

I walked resolutely now, retracing my steps back to the turn in the road. As I stepped around a dirty cloth on the ground – my mind registered it as a long stocking, woolen, army green - I heard a voice in front of me and raised my head.

It was Ram Aasray – my new friend in this time. '*Bhaiya ji*!' He repeated louder and waved his hand. I was at my turn now but had no option but to approach his stall under the Banyan tree. 'did you leave this behind?' He asked from a few feet away and raised his hand again – there was a small writing pad in it. I started shaking my head and heard myself say, 'that other man who had come? Remember, he went that way.' He slapped his forehead with the palm of his other hand. 'Yes, it must be his...' I offered solace, 'keep it with you, he will definitely come back. Otherwise...' I smiled and gestured that he cannot be expected to do more than that.

There was a pause now, as Ram Aasray and I stood quietly, waiting for something to break the lull. I was finding it difficult to start walking away – what if he sees where I am going? What if he follows me?

'Have you returned from some *videsh, bhaiya*?' His mumbled question took me by surprise, and all I could do was smile while shaking my head to reply in the negative; 'why did you think **that**?'

Before he could verbalize why he thought I was "foreign-returned", I noticed a family walking down the road from the other side. A tall, lean man, with a much-shorter elegant woman - an infant in her arms - and a toddler walking next to them. Dressed simply in plain clothing, obviously middle-class, and an ineffable air of peace around them. They were approaching the stall tentatively, and - with an unexplained difficulty – I peeled my eyes away.

As Ram Aasray moved towards them, I shook my head and turned around. Hope going back is as easy as entering this world!! Colonel Rana would be waiting for my report. Something, though, was pulling me back. Spend a few more minutes; a voice was murmuring in my head. The sunlight is much brighter here, it was whispering to me, why not enjoy it a bit more. I smiled inwardly at these voices, and kept going, back where I belonged.

The thought comes to me now, as I am writing this down; that perhaps this is what one might feel if wearing a virtual reality headset, or perhaps even playing in a reality show under the all-pervasive presence of closed-circuit TV cameras. As if the external world was less real than your personal world. Your inner worlds, extending till your appearance, your personal sphere, had sharpened; while the rest had become fuzzier, even malleable somehow, under your command.

CHAPTER III

21/11/15 - 22/11/15

[Saturday, 21/11/2015, 11PM]

I was on the verge of panicking again, by the time I got down from the side street and opened the ramshackle gate into the garden. What if I run into someone (that unseen person in the pump house), or what if I am not able to find the wall and the portal in it!? To calm myself, I deliberately slowed down and went through the makeshift gate carefully. The clearing was still unoccupied, but the towel was gone from the rope. I did not dwell on this, and crossed the clearing quickly. A few feet further on, and I observed the shrub I had seen before (the one with the flock of birds) and felt relieved that I was on track. With my head down, desperately concentrating on the task of returning home now, I realized that I have never missed my rented room this much before. I was so preoccupied with these thoughts that I almost crossed the wall, which was slightly more to the left than I remembered.

Chance now to test if this time-travel miracle works in reverse or not. I did not wait this time around, and in one quick motion was under the gate and out - back in the present, my heart hammering! It was the same as I had left it, thankfully.

I stumbled across the old grove – trees with an air of neglect around them, and walked to the opening in the wall that faced Faizabad road. Sidling out from this opening, my pulse beating fast, I stood for a second behind the Ashok tree which was hiding the opening, and peeped out at Faizabad road – in all its chaotic glory. Late afternoon traffic on a Saturday still seemed too much to bear. It looked like I was back. I had travelled back in time and returned in one piece! At least without any visible signs of physical transformation.

Getting onto the Faizabad road now, heading towards the IT Chauraha, I wondered what time it was. I had not worn a watch – based on instructions - and my phone had powered off. I turned it back on now – the bitten-apple logo appeared, and after a few seconds...lo, I was back in my time – 4:12 PM on 21 November, 2015. I was not sure, but my internal clock told me that about 25-30 minutes had passed. The mobile network bars appeared, and I looked around with more confidence. The IT College gate was grand but shabby, with scooters, motorcycles parked around in abandon. Crowds of people – from my time – in multi-coloured cloths, jeans, desperation, aggression. I could already notice the dust in the air much more clearly now. Even with the relief of being back, I discovered that walking was not easy – I felt drained – and so I decided to splurge on an auto-rickshaw to take me to Col Ranveer Rana's bunglow – my home. There was one driver standing next to his vehicle, and I remembered having seen him when I had come this way earlier. He had been talking on his mobile then, lounging with one foot up on the seat, and he was still in the same position. There was no mistaking his dark red tilak, the thick moustache, and the saffron flag tied to his side-mirror. Anyway, when he raised his eyebrows at me, I asked him to take me to "...near Nirala Nagar Post Office", and got in. In no mood to haggle about the price. As we lurched forward through traffic, I could not relax back on the seat, and slouched forward instead, with a hand clutching the vertical bar. I noticed the familiar landmarks pass me by, and imagined coming back here again some fifty years ago. Suddenly, 'Huh', as I realized that the driver was asking me something. He repeated grudgingly, 'nothing..., only asking; you came back from there so soon. All work done?' I froze on my seat, as my mind grappled with the thought that someone knew where I had gone! 'So soon? what do you mean...' I could manage that much. He laughed while he drove, and – '*Arrey*! No, I just saw you cross the *chauraha* and go towards college. *Bas*. And then you came back in five minutes, not even, so..., just asked.'

I felt relieved, at least partially, that he had not followed me to the garden. But, five minutes?! How is that possible? I looked out and noticed the Ramakrishna Mission gate, and could only wonder if this existed then – in 1966? There was so much to research!!

After a few more minutes of riding, while I came to grips with my present, I told him to turn right near the park, and we stopped at the fourth house. As I got out and paid, I felt thirsty, and slightly dizzy. Had to get inside, and off my feet for some time. I went directly to my room - walking in a dream now. My hand found the keys in my pocket, it went into the lock, and then I was inside. A swig of water directly from a bottle sitting next to the water filter, and I clumped down on the bed. But then my bile rose, and I had to run to the washbasin to throw up violently. The vomit was thin and painful, and left me shaking. I washed my face, and returned to bed. And then, 'Shit!' phone charging is a tough mistress, and I had to stretch to plug my phone in the charger next to the bed. Back on the bed now, lying down, head on the pillow, was but a moment's job, and sleeping off was even easier.

I woke up with a start, and groggily touched the phone to see the time. It was 6:20. Still the same day – though this may already be the strangest day I had experienced in my life yet! Should go meet the Colonel – this was my next thought. Another quick splash of water on the face, and a contemplative change of clothes - into my usual jeans and sweatshirt - and I went out again to face the world and to make my report. Will call Raju later, I told myself, though I did not think – even then – that I would mention any of this to him.

As I knocked on the door of the main house, it came to me that it was just 24 hours ago that I was standing here, waiting to talk to the Colonel about my rental agreement. The thought made me grimace widely, and just then a man opened the door. He looked at my still-smiling face with surprise, but – such is the human conditioning – could not help smiling back. Fair, thin and dressed in an old pair of track-pants and a worn-down blue t-shirt. He gestured for me to enter, and I followed him inside, as he turned into the kitchen and I continued on to the living room – where Colonel Rana was sitting.

He raised his hand in a kind of wave, and suggested, 'let us talk in English. Don't want that chap gossiping about this elsewhere.' I nodded and sat down, and he continued, 'did you make the trip? Are you ok, son?' This last was added, perhaps because he had seen something in my face.

'Yes, sir. I made the trip, as you call it! I don't know where I went when I passed under that hole in the wall, but it was exactly as you described. So, even though I still find it impossible, I guess I have to believe you.' He nodded with a face that was eager but trying to keep it in control. In the silence, we could hear some sounds from the kitchen, and then the smell of spices (black pepper?) and of onion.

'I will tell you the details in a minute, but first I have to confess – I had some tea there, and I vomited it after coming back. I was feeling very tired already, so after that I just slept off.'

'Understandable, Arjun. All of it. And I really appreciate you going on this trial mission. Do not worry about the tea, though. I don't think it would affect you – the human body is very resilient – especially when you are young!'

He called out to the cook then, asking him in hindi if the soup was ready. He came to the door to reply in the affirmative. Colonel looked at me, and then asked him to get two bowls for us.

'Now tell me – did you see her? And the man she was talking to?' His face turned wistful, and actually a little too sad to look at. Anyway, I composed myself and related the sequence of events from my visit to the past. In between, we got our soups and started sipping. It tasted great – hot and freshly prepared with carrots, tomato, onion, peas and lots of cathartic spices. I finished the story at the point where I had paid Ram Asray for the tea. He listened intently, and perhaps the soup, which he was also drinking heartily, kept him from interjecting or asking questions.

'...then I took a quick walk up to the IT College gate, and turned around and came back inside the garden, and through the gate – back here. There was some panic, when I thought I had lost my way, but I made it.'

I stopped and grimaced. Besides what I had related, I had been called a "foreigner", had experienced the IT College gate in that strange sunlight, and then that dapper man on the scooter, and (my eyes felt painful at the memory) that family of four just as I was leaving. But I kept those things inside, for now. I had to hear more about his experiences first.

He kept his soup bowl down on the table, and wiped his mouth with his hand. The cook reappeared, announced that the dinner was on the counter, and that he was leaving. The colonel looked at him, nodded, and he left quietly.

'First things first. You believe me now – right?' I nodded my agreement while slurping greedily at the soup. It was really good, helping calm my stomach (and my nerves) down.

'Ram Asray?' He chuckled, 'I never got his name during my visits! And of course, never tried his tea. Anyway, you saw them – Nalini and Mohan? What was your opinion of the encounter?'

Ah, so that was her name! It matched, somehow, with her appearance.

'I don't really know what to say. You had told me that this is what I will see, and I did. From my limited viewing, they could be friends, or relatives, or something else. Difficult to say. They were obviously important to you then, so I guess the actual mission is linked to them.' And then a thought struck me suddenly – 'is she..., was she, your wife, Colonel saheb?' I whispered, awed by my own imagination.

He was staring at me, though only with his eyes, I realized. Slowly, his thoughts came back to the present, and he shook his head briefly, 'No. And that was the problem. Let me finish my questions first. Debriefing's rules, you know!' He smiled twistedly at his vanity.

'Ok, next – did anyone notice you as being an outsider? Anything in your appearance, or in your interaction, that was so out of place that people might have noticed?'

It was my turn to smile – 'of course! All the time I was there, I felt like I was on a stage, and everyone was looking at me. But seriously, except for Ram Asray asking me if I was a foreigner, I think it went smoothly. Is it really important, though?'

'It is! In your actual mission you have to completely blend in. Part of the scenery, so to speak.' His mind was still intent on the task, obviously. 'We don't want you to be captured and handed over the police as a suspected "pakistani spy", right? If I remember correctly, our society at that time was highly sensitive to outsiders, or people who look and talk different!'

Maybe he was right, but my impression during the brief sojourn was that people also seemed more trusting, and less likely to make the mental jump from a "stranger" to a "pakistani spy". I did not argue with him, though, and just nodded vaguely. He should know better, right?

'Finally, about the timing. As I told you before, one thing is sure - that every time you go through that gate, it is about half-past three on 9 November, 1966. What I am less sure about is the time elapsed here while you are gone.'

'Yes, I noticed that too! I was not wearing my watch, so could not see the time, but when I came back to the IT *Chauraha*, this auto driver told me that I was only gone for about 5 minutes. But that much time would be spent on just walking from there to the wall inside the garden and then back! Even if that guy was useless at estimating the passage of time, I thought I was on the other side for at least 25-30 minutes. So....' I sputtered to a stop.

'My best estimate is that the time lapse in the present is only a few seconds. It may also depend on how long you are there for, for all I know. I was never gone for more than an hour, and actually measured my absence the last time (by leaving behind a running stop watch near the wall). It was less than 50 seconds!"

Leaving a running stop watch behind – this man was something! And as my mind tried to comprehend the complexities of time-travel, he continued.

'Since you will be going for a longer time, at least a few months, the time lapsed here may change, but I am sure it would still be short enough that no one is going to miss you here. It would be like you went for a piss inside that mango grove, and that's all.' He laughed loudly at his own imagination, but I did not join him – I was actually thinking of the length of time I would be spending in the past to complete the mission, and the fact that I did not know anything about it yet. That sobered me down. His laughter had turned into a bout of coughing, and my expression must have had an effect too, because he quietened down.

'Time can be a bastard, right? It weighs heavily like bricks in your backpack sometimes. And other times..., like a free fall, without a bloody parachute!'

He was sounding bitter, and not really in the mood for philosophical ruminations, I thought of trying some gentle distraction.

'Definitely, Colonel saheb. Should I get you some water? Or, if you are hungry...' I got up and stretched my back. It felt stiff, and so did my neck. He agreed to have some water, and I went into the kitchen to get it. I drank some first, and then, pouring the water from a bottle for him, I checked the casseroles kept there – thin, *khichdi*-like gruel, boiled vegetables; and... *kheer*! At least he will get his dessert.

He drank thirstily from the tumbler, and I sat back down – trying to imagine how regretful you have to be that you would want to change the past! Of course, he was doing it because this wonderful gate had opened up for him, and given him the opportunity – as he had said. And, as far I had known till yesterday, human lives do not get this option, and so they just accept their lot and continue. Or maybe give up on life itself, if it becomes really difficult to continue.

'Do you feel okay to talk more, Colonel saheb? I still have to learn so much more about this... this situation, but...!' This "but" emcompassed his health, dinner time and mental state in one word, though I need not have bothered.

'Sit down for a little while. I do not have much time left.' I sat down now, eager but worried by the seeming enormity of the situation I had found myself in. His voice was firm again.

'I will start with Sanju - my son Sanjiv - whom I failed completely. Already sensitive and thoughtful from the beginning, he went further into his shell after the death of his mother. I could not control anything. And the fact is, all I ever did was to try and control things and people. Never tried to understand. Anyway, he drifted around, till finally, around Christmas time in 2013, he came to me and told this story about a time-travel portal, which he had gone through and seen the other side!'

He wiped his face under cover of the shadows. The lamp was behind him, I could not see properly. But I was sure he was crying. I waited.

'I did not believe him at all, and I think I may even have laughed at him – telling him to get his head examined. I was responsible enough though, to actually try that, by taking him to a psychiatrist for a visit. Some chap in Gomti Nagar.' Colonel Rana shook his head in anger, his voice biting himself.

'Nothing helped. And..., and Sanju went through the gate again a couple of months later, and after returning from there, he got into bed, and never got out of it.' He paused for a few seconds, gripped his hands tightly, his eyes closed, as if praying. I waited.

'Anyway! Before he ..., left us, my boy told me everything. And as I heard his incoherant but astounding story, I decided to believe him finally. When he was on his death bed! Too late for all that..., but the more I brooded about coulds and woulds, it became clear to me that in outliving these two souls - one of whom would not have been born, if I had not married the other - I have done a terrible wrong! If only that accident had not happened, and if I had been a little better person, I would not have lost the true love of my life, and not marched into another marriage as a last resort and would not have helped bring Sanju into the world. I lost all of them, of course.

As I absorbed Sanju's experiences and his sorrow, and looked at my own life closely, I started seeing the possibilities. And I followed his footsteps into the past to check for myself. The obvious course of action came to me the first time I slipped back into 1966.'

He drank some more of the water, waved me back to my seat, since I had started getting restless, and continued.

'It was simple enough. If I can stay there in the past for a few months, I can undo the course of events which were triggered by that, that totally avoidable accident that resulted in ... death! So, I started preparing, and every visit to 1966 was like a mission for me. But I dwelt on it too much, in fact over-prepared myself till it slowly came to me that I will not be able to do it myself. And just as I was giving up on this ..., this dream, I found you!'

My mind was reeling. Where have I landed myself? Out of all the gloominess, what had really jumped out at me was that my mission was to stop a death from happening; now how would I do that!! As I grappled with this in silence, he must have seen some of my turmoil on my face.

'I know...., this is the sad and dirty little story of my family life. But before you jump to any conclusion, think about one thing, Arjun. If you help me now, we can undo all of it! ALL of it.' That made sense, but still – how do I stop death?! He was now gesturing at something under the coffee table.

'Pick up that briefcase, please. It has all the research and things I have collected. If you open it – there is a brown envelope on top – those are pages that Sanju was writing over his last few months. Take them with you tonight, read them, and let us meet again tomorrow.'

'But, Colonel Saheb – how do you expect me to stop someone from dying? Is that even possible?' I was beseeching him to understand the enormity of what he was asking me to do.

'Son, I know it seems difficult, even impossible. But I have a plan for that. I will tell you all about it, and believe me; you will not be directly preventing the death; all you have to do is to ensure that some people do not get together at the wrong place at the wrong time! That's all. You will understand when I tell you the details.'

I left him then, shaken inside, back to my room. Later at night I went through the motions, including calling up my "parents" on our weekly saturday-call, pretending as if everything was okay, making the usual conversation. I had dinner at a nearby restaurant – masala dosa and coffee – only things I could consider eating tonight. And all the while – on the road and at the restaurant, I continued to imagine how everything would have looked, way back in the year 1966!

Before I slept, I went through the pages – handwritten words documenting the descent into madness of a sensitive boy, who grew into a lonely, tormented man - Sanjiv Singh Rana. Lots of everyday tragedy captured on paper, like a lot of us do when we write a personal diary. But this had actually resulted in early death, and that was the real tragedy.

From what I could gather from the readings, Sanjiv was highly sensitive to the poverty outside, and the everyday pettiness he noticed among the comfortable existence of an upper-middle class home; he must also have noticed the distance between his mother and father. Slowly, he started believing that he really does not deserve his (at least materially) comfortable life. Drugs made their entry in his life then, though he was never explicit about what exactly, or how he dabbled in this addiction. And then, some kind of a messiah complex crept in – first ingrown, and then also fostered by his friends. He was very close to his mother, but she died early. He completed high school and Intermediate boards somehow (from Colvin College); though after a few wasted years. While others moved on and away, his friends and co-druggies, he stayed on, like an ardent party-goer who refuses to leave even when it is all over. A few years of silence, and then a late, out-of-turn admission at the Lucknow University, then his love for a much-younger girl in class, who did some "mental experiments" on him. He was vague about the details, but she apparently sent him on a wild-goose chase inside Chand Bagh. And this is where he stumbled across the portal into the past. His description of this trip was quite vivid, though more focused-on nature than the people. I also think he went around a bit, and not just towards Faizabad road. He also mentioned a temple where he meditated for a long time. Anyway, when he returned, he tried to tell all this to his father, but they had grown too far apart already, and his experience and story was not believed, of course. Sanju also spoke about how good it would be to go and live in the past. But this intention never went further – and I guessed his dependence on drugs must have stopped him. Finally, another time trip, combined with a drug trip, and his thoughts – and his life - went completely incoherent and confusing. My understanding was that a combination of his sensitive nature, the drugs, the disconnect within the family, and finally the heartbreak, all this was tipped over the edge by time-travels. He passed away in March 2014, at the age of 35!

• • •

[<u>Sunday, 22/11/2015, 8PM</u>]

After all the events of the last two days, my dreams last night were understandably confused and jumbled, and I remained hung-over in the morning. But then, over tea and the Sunday newspaper, I slowly regained my natural optimism. Being young and healthy helped, I am sure. On top of that, the prospect of the sizeable amount of money coming my way made it much more bearable, even attractive, in the morning. Yes, life can be tragic, but such tragedies are rare, and could easily be observed dispassionately when they do not touch you directly.

The strongest, most positive perspective came to me after I finished bathing. Admittedly, the Rana family has been in deep shit for decades, but I have the chance to make things right for everyone involved. It is "I" who will make the difference! The heroic possibilities fit in well with the bright sunlight of this Sunday morning. Spending a few months in a new place would be difficult, of course, but I thought I would be able to manage; with some help from Colonel Rana's preparations, of course.

I drank some milk (cold), ate a banana (slowly turning black), then dressed and went over to meet the Colonel again. Time to hear of his plan. I carried the tragic notes with me, just in case he wanted them back. And I forgot to call Raju again.

CHAPTER IV

22/11/15

[Sunday, 22/11/2015, 10PM]

Once more slipping through the gap in the hedge, hidden from the road by a tree, I moved quickly across the garden and to the wall with the opening in it. How the hell did this portal open here (and when), I was wondering - not the first rearing of this thought - but I had no clue where to even start looking, so brought myself back to the present. I had struggled a while to decide on the dressing this time, pulled between my comfort-wear and the consideration to avoid being out-of-place (and -time). Finally, I wore the same trousers, but pulled on a plain grey collared-tee, and made sure to leave my phone at home this time. It was later in the afternoon, and I was going for another round of time-travel. To go through another test Colonel Rana had devised – a big test, it seemed like – though I also wanted to do some explorations of my own.

I was trying to stay focused on this trip so much and had psyched myself up enough, that as soon as I reached the wall, I came to a stumbling stop. The small opening suddenly seemed like a block to my progress. I took a deep breath, remembered that it was not really a block, and bent down to squat through.

It felt like the exact same moment as my last entry; but how could I be sure, after all? The bright sunlight, the wilderness of trees, the bright green of shrubs, along with a singular lack of clutter. Perhaps I walked quicker this time around, because I noticed the birds scattering off and resettling from the corner of my eye and turned around to verify. Through to the clearing, the towel swinging a bit on its rope, and then on to the wooden gate in the hedge, and out on the road. I turned my head quickly to take in the withdrawing bullock cart, walked carefully around the dung heap, and glanced briefly up at the cyclist as he passed by. It was great to know what is going to happen, but I could not let go of the worry that it may probably be very fragile, because just the fact that I was here may be screwing things up.

Reaching the Faizabad Road, I only took a quick look towards Ram Aasray, and made sure the “drama” was still happening on the road, before turning to the right and walking on towards IT College after crossing the road quickly. Ah, you see now the sneaky plan I had in mind? Yes, I will go to the *Chauraha* and bide my time till the lady came by in her rickshaw. I will then follow her in another one. When describing the critical “test”, Colonel Rana had said that I will have more than 20 minutes to reach the railway crossing towards Nishatganj, so I knew I could afford some explorations of my own. At least for a while the “test-case” could continue to breath.

Feeling self-congratulatory already, I reached the IT *Chauraha*; this time with just a quick appreciative glance towards the riot of colors at the College gate (“*jeevan se lambe hain...*”, really!) I had kept to the left side while walking, and when I checked again, I saw her ride coming, the wheel-rims glinting in the sunlight. Then I realized a problem - I had no idea which way she would go. There were three options, and if she turned right, I would have to cross the road towards that side. There were only two rickshaws I could notice – one standing on the far side, towards Daliganj, and one close to where I was. Turning my head again, I saw her rickshaw coming straight, and decided to catch one for myself. I glanced at it – driver leaning back on his seat, counting his coins and placing them in a small cloth bag tied to his waist; a *dhoti*, a *kurta*, a black shawl around his neck; brown skin, an old scar on the side of the cheek, tired eyes. I heaved myself up on to the unexpectedly high seat. 'Let us go', I said in Hindi, trying to sound as normal as possible. He turned around and asked gently, 'where, *babu*?' Her rickshaw passed by just then, the rotations slowing down at the crossing, and then going straight towards Daliganj and beyond. I lifted my hand and directed him in Hindi, 'straight.' We started out on my first rickshaw chase ever. As we crossed the *Chauraha*, for some reason I remembered the scooter rider with sunglasses, who would be coming from behind us – but he was not due for another few minutes.

There we were then – tworickshaws, one behind the other and moving leisurely through the sparse traffic towards Daliganj. The seat behind the driver's perch had a comfortable back-support, but I still had to swivel my neck around the driver's back to make sure she was still ahead. I felt my hand grip the side-bar tighter, an irrational fear of falling clouding the mind. There were some buildings on both sides of the road, houses and shops, and most looked gray and unpainted. Some pedestrian traffic, as usual, and lots of cyclists. It felt like a small town, and the wind on my face felt clean. Less dust, and no mobile recharge/repair stores, cyber-cafes or fast-food restaurants – none of the detritus of 21st Century urban India. Among the plainness, I noticed a small shop front, with magazines and newspapers hanging on ropes, and made a mental note to come back for some browsing.

Just beyond that stall, the rickshaw in front turned right (for a moment I could see her profile – it still glowed over the distance), and I asked my driver to turn too. There was a small park-like space to our left now, and it struck me then, that if we keep going on this road, perhaps we will reach Nirala Nagar, somewhere close to where I stay – back in 2015! Then I saw her stop, and I asked my driver to slow down. She got down carefully – straightening the kurta behind her, adjusting the bag in her hands – and walked into a doorway. As we passed by, I read the board above – written in Urdu and Hindi scripts – "Nisar Ahmed". I stopped my transport a few meters ahead and searched for change in my pocket. The rickshaw-wala was smiling at me, but I did not encourage his invitation for exchanging confidences. 'How much?' I asked, almost brusquely, and he replied, subdued now, '*dus naya paisa*.' Relieved (I had the correct change) I handed over two 5-paise coins, and turned around, walking towards the doorway. I assumed it would be a shop, but there was nothing outside to indicate what kind. There was a flour mill next to it, and I stood in front of that – inhaling the smell of freshly-ground wheat-flour – considering my next step, when the door opened, and two women came out of the shop, chatting in undertones while putting back some fabric inside their cloth bag. They were both wearing burkas, and appeared young and well-off. Must be a tailor, I concluded, and debated whether I should wait. My ride had already gone back and was out of sight now, but I noticed that her rickshaw was still there, waiting under a tree a few meters down the road – whether in hope or by instruction, I had no way of knowing. Loitering in this quiet street would only raise suspicion, and so I decided to walk back to the main road and try the newspaper shop I had seen. I felt sure (or maybe just hoped) she would come back this way after finishing her work at the tailor. The only problem now was that I was without a ride.

I had to walk with care, because there was no footpath – only a drain (sewer?) with flat stone slabs covering most of the gaps. I also had to keep turning around frequently to check in case she comes out. At the main road, I looked back once more before turning to my left. And there I was – a place where I could buy a newspaper. A sleepy middle-aged man was sitting behind the stall – with round eye-glasses, a cap covering his head, and a sullen expression. Which made it easier for me to avoid conversation, as I browsed the selection, and picked up a newspaper (The Pioneer) and a Hindi magazine (Dharmayug) and looked inside. There were no English magazines I could see, and the Dharmayug was really expensive (65 NP) considering everything else, but still felt like a good deal to me. No buying anything right now, though!

Not wanting to make the unhappy gentleman too annoyed, I left the reading matter behind, and decided to go back. Walking back slowly on the other side of the street from the Tailor. Somebody up there must have estimated the timing to perfection, because just as I was crossing the shop, she came out. Our eyes met, and then she looked down while adjusting her dupatta over her head. Nice strong chin, full mouth, and large confident eyes above a sharp-but-not-proud nose. I mentally corrected my earlier impression – she does not really look "too tough!" As I walked on, I noticed that she had also turned to her right, so now we were walking parallel to each other. I tried hard not to look towards her. Reaching the rickshaw first, I asked him in a low voice – 'are you free?' The man was reclining on the seat, with his hands clasped behind his head, his eyes closed and his lips moving – chanting a mantra or something, I guessed. He opened his eyes and turned around at my voice, but then he also noticed the girl approaching on the other side and got up in a hurry. '*Mem Saheb*?' He spoke up – loud but respectful – and she just shook her head from the other side of the street, a hint of a smile on her face. The rickshaw-wala and I watched her as she continued on her way, the bag swinging by her side. Ah well! We finally turned away and faced each other. 'where to take you, saheb?' He was standing on the ground now, a hand on the rickshaw-handle while patiently waiting for me to reach a decision.

'Nishatganj', I answered shortly and climbed up. Nalini was crossing the street and while turning once (to check traffic perhaps - though there was no real need for that) glanced towards me. And then she was gone, almost skipping the last few steps towards a house that was at the dead-end of this street.

I breathed out and turned around, as the rickshaw started moving towards the main road. Tried to relax and bring my thoughts back to what the Colonel had told me.

['...later that afternoon, Mohan had come to my house in New Hyderabad, where I was in bed recovering from fever and cold. I still remember his glee, his insufferable mirth, when he came. Maybe it was because of Nalini, but at that time I mixed it up with my sickness. I even remember hating him for it! Anyway, you do not have to follow him, because there is something even more important for you to do. And this will tell us if what we are trying to do is even possible, or is it all futile.

On my second trip back to that day, I had walked towards Nishatganj, and while waiting at the railway crossing, witnessed a street dog getting under a train. You have to - somehow - save that dog from getting killed. I have told you the scenario, as I understood it, and if you can avert this small accident, it will tell us that perhaps it is possible to do this at a larger scale too. And I am sure it will also give you some confidence; like a dress rehearsal.']

In my rickshaw, we were crossing the IT *Chauraha* again and waited to let a large car pass. There were three people sitting in the car, their elbows hanging outside the window, blank eyes gazing around, as if in wonder of the ride itself. It felt kind of enormous that I was the only one around who was aware of a minor accident about to happen nearby; in just a few minutes.

And then we were moving again, crossing the IT College gate with the flowers gleaming brightly in the afternoon sunlight, the thick hedge covering the garden of time-travel next to it, then Ram Asray's stall (I could not help looking towards it, but he was crouched down and fiddling with the earthen stove), and then we were on the open road, with trees on the left and some scattered building on the right. I did not see that family from last time, and perhaps it was just as well. There was something really disturbing about that memory, even though I could not put my finger on why that would be so. Moving along slowly, a green flag captured my attention – a *mazaar* (tomb) of some saint behind it. Don't think it exists in 2015. Or perhaps it has just been well-hidden.

Now I could make out the railway crossing in front, with a drop gate, which was closed already. I told the driver to stop and paid off, telling him that I will walk to Nishatganj, no problem, etc. I could see the gray building of Fatima Hospital, but it was on the other side of the crossing. Right where I had gotten down from the rickshaw, I noticed a ramshackle stall on the road. Smaller than Ram Asray's, and with no tree to locate itself under. It was leaning against the boundary wall of a property that did not appear to be under construction.

What now: any dogs around? Yes, there was one trotting towards me, its coat grimy, but eyes bright as a healthy baby's, and its tail wagged as it saw me. I have never particularly liked the friendliness of dogs, so it was easy to disregard him, as it crossed me and went on its way. Looking around, I noticed another dog – this may be the one! It was sleeping next to the railway track, in a depression in the ground, adjacent to a large rock, and even in the shadow where it was sleeping, I could make out the black coat and the prominent white mark on its forehead. Now, what was it that the Colonel had told me – as the train approaches, something or someone will cause the dog to wake up with a start, and also cause the panic that will make him run suddenly – right under the wheels of the train.

I heard the distant sound of a train now, and as I watched, some pedestrians went under the railway gate and crossed the tracks. They were in no particular hurry, as if used to this; some things never change! I looked around at the people waiting on the other side, including a *Tonga* – a horse-driven cart - with an old man sitting primly in it, stopped a few feet from the gate. I still had no clue yet on what could cause that sleeping dog to panic and run under the train.

I moved closer to the stall and noticed a few people under the lean-to shade. One older man stirring a vessel (tea, probably?) and two boys, in clean but hand-me-down shorts and shirts, crouching on the ground, playing with something, though with their backs to me, I could not really see what. The sound of the train was now louder, and as I desperately searched for a solution to the problem (which was not yet a problem), I had a brainwave. Striding quickly across the road, I went to the sleeping dog, positioned myself in front (so that I was between it and the railway track) and shooed – trying to wake it up. No reaction, and I had no option but to shout loudly – "*hutt*!" and stamp my foot on the ground – hard. The dog woke up with a start and bestowed me with a dazed look. Disregarding the frown from the old man in the *Tonga*, I waved my hands, till finally the dog got up on its front legs – still sleepy and disinterested but perhaps realizing my desperation – and walked slowly, away from the tracks, and down the road. The train was almost upon us and gave out a loud whistle. I jumped – taken by surprise – and saw that the dog also gave a start. But it was well away from the train now, and safe for the time being.

As the train clattered by next to us, the sound and vibrations almost unbearable to me, I noticed that the boys at the stall were standing up and throwing something at it. A small stone whizzed by and hit the rock – right where the dog had been sleeping. Aah! This is what must have happened then – if I had not shooed the dog away – I realized and sighed with relief. I could read the sign – Gorakhpur Express, in Hindi – on the side of the coaches of the train, which seemed to be all general class; no sealed dark windows of the Air-conditioned coaches yet; passengers looking out from the windows, lazily observing the people gathered at the crossing. One of them shouted something at the boys throwing the pebble. The boys shouted back, safe in their own stationery world, as the train went past. And then it was gone, leaving quietness behind, and only the clatter of the wheels in the air.

I turned and started walking back the way I had come. No reason for me to cross over to the other side of the railway track yet. The black dog whose life I had saved, had made itself comfortable again by the side of the road, and was ready to go back to sleep. As I passed by, it raised its head a little and looked at me – neutral, but circumspect - and I whispered – 'you are welcome!'

What now? I had fulfilled one task, without much difficulty either, and that did give me confidence. Perhaps more than I had a right to feel, but it was enough to make my walk jaunty as I strolled on Faizabad road towards my destination. The road was narrower than it would later become, but the sides ended in a grassy strip which – though not totally flat – was still walkable. Pedestrians were mostly walking on the tarred surface itself, though. In terms of traffic, they have no idea what is coming, I thought and grimaced. Passing by the *mazaar* now, I realized something – I will have to come and do this next time around as well! Make sure I remember, otherwise the dog will die. Again. My head started aching at the thought. And when I go back to the present this time – would anything have changed there. Because of a street dog who is now going to live longer than it actually had. Till this fucking gate, and Colonel Ranveer Rana, (and I, of course), came around and decided to screw up the passage of time!!

My mood had turned inexplicably angry, and I mouthed a "Shit!" just as a little girl and her father crossed me on the road. The man was somber-looking, wearing loose pajama and kurta, and had close-cropped hair – with a wispy top-knot – hanging at the back. The girl was little, about 6 or 7, her hair oiled and tied in braids, a long skirt and a top, once yellow but faded now, and her *kaajal*-lined eyes were on me when the "shit" came out. She gave a visible start and started crying! She also stopped on the road, as her father came out of his reverie and tried to mollify her. I stopped too, unsure of whether I could be of any help. After the first shriek, her cries were more like whimpers now, and the father seemed to be managing well. I continued walking, with a consoling thought leading me on – that I have already done enough for the day.

If only I had my earphones with me; some music, perhaps. But – let us focus and do a headcount. Who is where right now, in this version of the past? The about-to-die-in-4-months Mohan has taken a rickshaw to meet the yet-to-be Colonel, who is recovering from illness at home. Nalini "*devi*" has reached home (and I know where it is – already!) That sickly black dog must have slept off again, not knowing (and does it matter?) that it could have died a few minutes ago. Ram Aasray must be at his stall, and I have to cross him to get to that Garden-from-hell! So that I can travel back to my life in 2015. My life, which is slipping away, as surely as the feel of the road under my sandals. The next time I come here, I will have to find a way of getting into the lives of some of these people. Though Colonel Rana claims he has a plan, I wonder. Unsurmountable opportunities? That is how it appears.

Deep in thought, with my hands in my pockets, I reached the tea stall under the tree, and would have passed by without stopping, except that a memory came back to me from my last visit. Shaking my head with pleasure at it, and the idea it had engendered, I approached Ram Aasray, and called out cheerfully, 'can I get some chai here?' He looked exactly the same (unsurprisingly), but the circumstances were a little different this time. He was more matter of fact now, not in the mood for chit-chat, and I moved towards the tabular structure next to the tree trunk where Mohan would had stood earlier and smoked his cigarette. Next to a large clay pot and a metal trunk, I saw it. The small writing pad that Mohan had left behind, and which Ram Aasray had thought was mine when I was here last time. In the "original" past (and I could only guess) the pad was left behind, and then perhaps reclaimed by Mohan later. If every visit to the past was a reset, the next time I come (and leave it alone), Mohan can return and claim it. Only problem is that there will then be two such pads, one written till today which I am picking up, and the second one in which Mohan will continue to write till he is able to. Before I would allow myself to be completely entangled in these thoughts, I picked the pad quickly and pushed it in my belt at the back.

I turned around casually, and stepped towards Ram Aasray, who was pouring tea in a kulhad. The steam rose from it, and I handled it gingerly, blowing at it lightly. I remembered the taste from yesterday (or was it today, just a few minutes ago?), and I also knew that he was from Varanasi. Thoughts whirling in my head and making sure I do not turn my back towards him, I asked him if he knew which day it was. I used the Hindi word "*din*", and he must have misunderstood, because he actually had to give it some thought – 'today, hmmm? Tomorrow is *dhanteras*, so today must be *Dwadashi*.' And then he added half-smilingly, 'Diwali is almost here, bhaiya ji.'

He was referring to the Hindu Lunar calendar, of course. And, of all the weeks of the year, the time-travel portal had to land us here in the week of Diwali! I could just sip at the tea in silence. The Colonel could not have missed this, but he had not mentioned it either. Anyway, Ram Aasray was still waiting for some reaction from me, so I tried to be polite – 'on Diwali, you will go to your village?' I was trying to keep it casual and distant. He did not, though – 'what village? Now this is only my village, bhaiya!' And after a pause, 'family has to be fed', and a longer pause, with an air of finality, 'if only this shop becomes set...' I only nodded my head in sympathy, and paid him 10 *paise* (again), refusing to take any change in return.

I am screwed. This thought first came to me as I started walking slowly back from the past. My second trip, and it already seemed like I was being divided; parts of my mind, perhaps my whole self, were being left behind in 1966 with every trip. Going back was like walking in sand, as if this world was slowing my steps; the brighter light making me feel more concrete, significant, and even heavier than in my own world. All imaginary, I am sure, but then the strangeness of my experience had to justify some purpose, somehow!

I had reached the opening, and as I placed my hand on the makeshift gate to push it open, I felt something pierce my thumb. I sucked at the drop of blood thoughtfully as I walked in. My thoughts did not interfere in my walking though, and I was still sucking it when I went through and returned to the present – with Mohan's writing pad with me.

Did not really feel like going back to meet the Colonel after returning today. But I had to report whatever was achieved today. So, I did go and meet him later in the evening. He looks weaker already, but still has some energy left to take an interest in the plan. How does he manage to keep his hope alive? The need for a better life is understandable, but this is grotesque! And what about my role in it?

This feels like a trap. A gilded cage, practically.

CHAPTER V

23/11/15 - 26/11/15

[Monday, 23/11/2015, 6:45PM]

After yesterday's excursion and exertions, today was different. There was much to do, of course, but more of mental efforts than physical exercises. Will meet the Colonel later today for another set of instructions. Hope to get some real stuff also – not just descriptions! The writing pad that I picked up (written by Mohan in 1966!!) was mostly filled with poetry - amateur, romantic, idealistic, along with some naked admissions of weakness or vanity or other sins. I felt ashamed reading it but accepted it as an occupational hazard now.

I went to the office, as a matter of routine, but did not really do any of the work for which I earned my salary. Wikipedia (and Google, in general) were my friends today. Oh, the sheer amount of information available on the most arcane topics is truly mind-boggling. I searched and read and watched so much my brain started bubbling. Found some old news videos from the 60's, about India and the world. Read about the politics, the popular hangouts, popular Hindi movies playing then, and Filmfare awards won. Who knew (I did not!) that an Indian girl had won the Miss Universe title in early 1966!!! Both the Prime Minister of the country and the Chief Minister of UP were women in November of that year! There were food riots in West Bengal, and Hindu-Sikh riots in Delhi. And an "attack" on the parliament by saints and their followers for cow protection! Punjab state got formed. Lucknow University faced student unrest and protests. Hanuman

Setu (aka Monkey Bridge) over the Gomti River was completed but would get inaugurated only in January 1967. Very helpfully, Wikipedia has pages listing major events, year-wise for India! I started looking at 1966, 1967, and then continued till the previous year. At the end of about 2 hours of this research and compilation, I had a list of most remarkable (and tragic) events of the last 50 years, with dates, casualties, impact, everything! Amazing.

My eyes were glazed as I left from office that evening and headed back home. Such as it was. I was trying not to think but could not shake off the feeling of fatigue that sometimes creeps on before the beginning of long journeys. There was not much packing to be done, which was a relief. The problem, besides the objective of this journey, of course, was the duration. I could be there for a few months, but when I return, it will be the same day here – only a little while later. At least that was what the Colonel and I thought. The co-conspirators!

"There is a tide in the affairs of men, which, when taken at the flood, leads on to fortune.' That was what Shakespeare had written, and I had believed, and I am sure I was not the only one to agree. Till the tide actually comes along, and that is when the wheat gets separated from the chaff. Or as the Hindi saying has it, "milk to milk, and water to water (get separated)." When faced with an actual tide, you realize what your inner strengths are, how strong your motivation really is! And a tide of such gigantic proportions!! I doubt many people in the world would have faced such a prospect. It was not a "life & death" situation (thanks a lot for that, though how could I be sure!), but the strangeness of the enterprise, and the scary nature of potential outcomes, was what made it so, so...difficult to put your brain around!

Then, like a blanket on a cold night, the thought of Colonel's crores covered me in a warm gift-wrap. The money that is to come to me at the end of it all. And as usual, the anticipation of riches made things a little easier, a bit more bearable.

And yes, I think I should meet Raju once. There is no way I can tell him the amazing story I find myself in, but... I am also not sure how I can avoid the topic completely, once we get talking.

But I know I will have to.

• • •

[Tuesday, 24/11/2015, 10PM]

Long discussion yesterday and today with Colonel Rana. Lot of background information shared, some food for thought, and pages to read, and notes to take. Good that I have taken leave from office for two days (for now). At least I am able to form a more solid image of the key players in this "drama":

Nalini – born in 1948 in the Shukla family of Chand Ganj, was about 2-year younger than our Colonel, and – of course – the love of his life. In the year 1966, she was studying for her BA degree at the IT College. When Mohan, a distant cousin (more about him below) died in an accident in early 1967, she tended to blame the Colonel (as he thinks), and went and married someone else (an arranged match) in 1970. Within 6 years, the marriage dissolved, and after the divorce, Nalini never married again, moved to Haridwar, and lost touch with everyone. In 2013, she passed away after a heart attack.

Mohan – A third-cousin of Nalini's, who was born and lived in Lucknow. A few months younger than the Colonel, little older than Nalini. In B. Com. final year at the Lucknow

University. Dies a stupid death on the banks of Gomti River (not too far from the Monkey Bridge) in March 1967, while the Colonel was distracted, and the newly-inaugurated bridge had watched on indifferently.

Colonel Ranveer Singh Rana – Born in Bareilly in 1947, studied there, and then at Lucknow University, got selected to join the army, but before joining, was involved – though not directly responsible for – Mohan's accidental death in 1967. Got married (to the future Mrs. Rana - already fragile, not yet sickly) in 1972, but became a father only later in life – 1979 - by which time Nalini had also divorced and moved away. Sanju's mother – which is how Rana always thought of her – slowly become sicker, and ultimately died of a pneumonia infection in 1997. He went into a deeper shell, and the son grew up on his own. Rana learnt of Nalini's death in 2013, Sanju died in 2014, and Rana went through the portal after that for the first time. And then a few more visits, and his plan was formed – with me as a pawn!

Finally, here is the event – as told by the Colonel – that I have to somehow, stop from happening:

Early afternoon of Saturday, March 25, 1967. The day before Holi. This is what Rana recalls –

Beautiful spring day, Amaltas and Gulmohar blooming; holidays on other people's minds, he imagines, though his own thoughts are focused on his military career and on his future with Nalini. He has gone through the SSB process, been selected, and would be leaving for the Military Academy in a few weeks. They had gone to watch some English movie at the Mayfair theatre. Mohan is with them, of course, along with another classmate of Nalini's, and he is happy enough with life to not complain at all during the entire movie. Nalini's friend (Ranveer does not remember her name) is engaged to be married already. Afterwards, perhaps buoyed by the movie-watching, or just happy to be out of the stuffy theatre, the four decide to walk Nalini's friend to her home in Kaiserbagh. No firm plans - will see what happens later. They reached the Y-junction where the Lakshman Park started and turned towards the right arm. Slow, lazy walk, not much talk, except Mohan's intermittent chatter, and then Begum Hazrat Mahal Park in front of them. He is eager to say it all to Nalini, is not sure of how to do it, though he feels confident she will reciprocate his emotions. He is definitely impatient though, by now. Another intersection in front; if you turn right, you cross the newly inaugurated Monkey Bridge - or Hanuman Setu - over the Gomti and reach University and IT *Chauraha.* Nalini and her friend turn left though, and Rana speaks up, surprising even himself, 'meet at the end of the park? Towards Chattar Manzil?' Nalini nods, but he waits for more, a look, some direct signal perhaps. She is moving faster now, and once across the road, turns around to look at him. '1 minute!' he growls at Mohan, who is saying something – as always! And keeps his eyes on her. She moves her right hand in a half-wave, and then a three-quarter roll. Bye, and will meet you down the road; that's how he interprets that! Rana smiles back, but perhaps not wide enough for her to be able to see from the distance. Then he is following Mohan, who is ahead, but slowing down. Then Mohan turns completely around, and addresses Rana – 'big brother, ever seen a twin-colored lotus?' Rana waves a derisive hand and tries to push forth. No KD Singh Babu Stadium then, nor Hotel Clarks Awadh; mostly bare ground, either open or with trees, as you moved closer to the Gomti River. The bare expense of Hazrat Mahal Park on their left, the top of the Chattar Manzil in front. No spire of the Shaheed Smarak pillar behind it then; it was not built yet. The sequence of events after this is blurred for Rana, or maybe he has tried to bury it deep. Mohan still talking about some exotic lotuses in a shallow of the Gomti River. He gets off the road on their right, and they walk around mounds of moist earth towards the river. Somehow, they are now arguing a topic that lends itself easily to throwing dares at each other - "what kind of limit (*hadd*!) would you cross for the love of your life?". Mohan keeps smiling from the side of his mouth, as if challenging him. And then a small pond, channeled from a secret tributary of the Gomti, and beautiful lotuses blooming in the middle. He could count at least three different shades of pink and white. About 20 feet inward from the muddy edges on their side. Rana has thrown a challenge – why doesn't Mohan prove his *hadd* by picking one lotus? He is also in love, isn't he? Mohan is thoughtful, lighting a cigarette as they stand near the edge. Rana wanting to go back to see Nalini and be with her. A creeping feeling of disgust with Mohan's presence! So much so that he lands a low challenge - "...if you're a man...", and starts walking back. Hearing a gentle splash after a few steps. Not turning around to check; feeling sure that it is another ploy by the melodramatic Mohan! And then those bubbling sounds (he seems to remember those very well), and turning around, sees the dark hair coming up once, and twice, and then the bubbles on the surface, disappearing in slow-motion, and him scared of going any farther (his feet are getting wet, the shoe-soles sticking to the ground). He shouts out, but it sounds like croaking, and then he is running back towards the main Hazratganj road, and he is sure it is too late, and finally there are people on bicycles, who follow him back, and then he sees Nalini. Does not dare go to her. She stands far in the back, as the crowds gather, and there is talk about people being foolhardy, and the feeling of guilt. Mostly. Also, (as Rana confessed now) because he is scared of water! The body is pulled out, and he tries to explain to everyone what had happened. No direct blame on him, even by the police, who finally label it an accidental death, and close the file.

So, this was the story of that fateful day, which - let us not forget - Rana now wants to erase. Wants me to erase, actually. Stop it from happening. Because, as he explains once more: Nalini would not marry him after that, holding him responsible, if not directly blaming him, for what had happened. Then she gets married – to someone else - and after half-dozen years undergoes a divorce. He has already been married by that time, and then years pass, and he becomes a father, and their paths have completely, irrevocably diverged....

In the evening, when we met again, the Colonel handed me a heavy gold chain. 30 gm, he said, and asked me to use it for the expenses of the trip. I asked him when I could start; he said that he will let me know soon. And he said, go to the Khunkhun ji Jewelers' shop in Aminabad, and give it as a collateral. What, I asked, now? You need money now? And he actually slapped his forehead - no... when you go through! You will need money in 1966-67, right? As I write, I have the chain in my left hand; and it feels comfortingly heavy.

I have to meet him again and get the decision done soon. Too much preparations, and not enough action!! But if I really start thinking about it, I am still not ready – how the hell can you prepare for something like this? About the chain – Rana suggests that I keep it as collateral with the jeweler, and in return, take some cash as advance, and work out some monthly payment for six months. I only have to be there for that duration, and towards the end, I can decide whether to leave the chain behind (when I come back), or use some of my saved/earned money to get it released. Even if they would want to, nobody from 1966 would be able to get hold of me once I am back in my time.

Time to indulge in some personal ruminations now. Only appropriate (and natural) to review your own life before such a huge transition, I guess. It is not easy to write about yourself, we all know that. Under normal circumstances. Which these are definitely not! Not by a long stretch. The defining characteristics: Arjun is 27, was adopted (just after his birth) by Mrs. Radha and Mr. Sharad Kumar Saxena in Allahabad in 1988, and then moved to Roorkee in 1999, when Mr Saxena moved with a new job in the accounts department at the University there. He completed his B.Sc. after schooling, got admission for a post-graduate degree in Geology, worked in Dehradun for a couple of years, and then came to Lucknow to join the Geological Survey of India in 2014. Only child, somewhat detached from society, family and friends – this “apartness” getting aggravated once he found out that he was actually adopted, and not born in the family. Likes *shayari* and music and books, is cynical and dismissive of most fads. So, when he meets Anjali in Hazratganj towards the end of 2014 (her cousin – and his colleague - Rajesh had introduced them), the falling in love is not something that comes naturally – but it happens, and after a few months of being on an emotional roller-coaster, a bitter – because sudden - end in October this year. The man (boy?) is not very ambitious, but open to new experiences (Anjali being one prominent example of that), and adventurous enough to hazard a trip to the past to save a life. A big motivation, of course, is the money that comes to him for doing this! Actually, he has already saved another life in the past – remember the dog – and can only wonder now what effect it might already have on the future.

Fine. That came out well, I think. Does not explain anything really, but it felt good to put it down on paper. The bottom-line is that perhaps no one else but yours truly could have taken up Colonel Rana's offer. Was my whole life leading up to it? That may be taking it too far.

Yes, also met Raju today for beer, and shared a bottle. And then a second. He was wondering why I am on leave, and I managed to convince him that it is only because I want to use up some of my balance days of leave. Talked of this and that, good-natured chit-chat with the beer helping the conversation, but managed to avoid the big story. And it seemed like the right thing to do.

It is late but will again go over my notes on the situation in 1960s-70s. After all, they are my survival pack for the time travel coming up soon. As is this gold chain!

• • •

[Wednesday, 25/11/2015, 8PM]

Colonel Ranveer Rana died in the early hours today.

I got to know of it from the sound of the ambulance that rolled into the gate just as I was finishing my obligatory cup of tea – still in my track pants and t-shirt (another day off from work!). I came down to check. It was late morning, and though I had thought of meeting the Colonel later, that will not happen now. I guess this is what he had meant last night that he will let me know soon. I met the lawyer, the middle-aged Advocate Satish Chandra. Not very expressive, but appeared competent, and mostly benign. It seemed the instructions were that he be called when something like this happened, and so he had come, leaving his other affairs behind to go through the last will of the Colonel, and do what needed to be done. Which he did, and we met, and he gave me a laconic and official summary. Half the property and cash in my name. Will bring some documentation in a day or two for signing, etc. Some curiosity shone through in the experienced eyes, atop the portly frame. But he did not delve into it today, thankfully, because he knows that I will be here for more heart-to-heart meetings. Where would I go after getting such a windfall – at least till the paperwork is all done.

• • •

[Thursday, 26/11/2015, 3PM]

I made up my mind right around lunch time and started packing the few things I was going to take. I must have had some moisture in my eyes by now, because the gold chain – as I again weighed it in my hand – looked fuzzy, the gold flowing and dissolving in my hand. Besides the chain, my notes about major events; coins and currency, some medication – for the short term – hopefully; two sets of extra clothes; some other odds & ends; including the very important certificates in the brown paper envelope; and finally, my mp3 music player with about 500 songs stored on it, along with earphones and a charger. And, of course, Mohan's writing pad! Might be of some use.

It is just after 3PM in the afternoon again. For some reason it feels appropriate, sort of a divine (?) rule, that I should cross the portal around the same time when I come out of it. Perhaps to minimize the jetlag. Ha-ha-ha!!! So, after I write down these final words, I will start out on my adventure.

I have decided one thing though; this diary will stay behind. I have no idea what effect my going to the past – and of changing it – is going to have. And I sure as hell want to have a written record of what had happened so far. So that when I come back, I can read it up and remember. Just in case...

There are many small questions, but only one big question: how much time would have passed here, when I come back through the gate after the 150 odd-days I spend in 1966-67?

Ahh, screw it. Enough of this vomiting on paper. Let's go!

Part 2: Memories come rushing

Friday afternoon. 18 March 2016. The old man places the diary down on the table next to him carefully; the faded pages almost falling apart now from within the tattered covers. His thoughts confused and stomach uneasy, he looks at the diary with something like disgust. Why did Ramesh have to bring this to him!?

There is a story here - about him and people he has known – but an altered version of reality! And who is this Arjun Saxena? He had known one Arjun Sharma – "the Opaque man" - who had come into their lives many years ago and disrupted his plans. At least temporarily. But he had then died.

And how can anyone write so much nonsense? There is a Time-portal in Chand-Bagh! I became a Colonel in the Indian army, and have already DIED last year in November!? And Mohan? He has been dead since 1966?!! In which world?!

Is it even possible that this is all his own doing – how things happened to him? To all of them!

Sitting in his Indira Nagar house, Ranveer Singh Rana allows himself, and memories wash over him.

CHAPTER VI

1966-1969

Rana is in the middle of a barren land. And then, a sudden, welcome arrival of rain on parched soil, and the exciting smell of freshly wetted earth. He felt drops on his forehead now...

It was actually sweat, slipping down to his temple, and he opened his eyes, and thought about the dream. Something HAS happened – this was his next thought. The fever was gone, and though the body was tired, his chest felt clearer and lighter. Rana turned his head on the pillow and faced the afternoon sunlight glowing through the thin curtains of the only window in the room. He wiped his mouth and face with his palm and sat up in bed. What has happened? The question lingered on his mind, like an annoying mosquito buzzing nearby.

There was a rude knock on the door, and a voice called out – 'elder brother!' Rana cursed under his breath and got out of bed. 'Coming', he shouted weakly, and went over to pour himself some water from the clay pot in the corner of the room. Sipping it slowly – it tasted bitter – he went over to the door and unshackled the chain above. The two panes of the door opened with some resistance, and he saw Mohan in front of him – grinning his trademark grin. There was a rickshaw behind him, turning around lazily in the street.

Mohan pushed past him cheerfully – 'possible to get some tea?'

'Where are you coming from? And no, no tea here!' Rana climbed back in bed and rested against the wall. 'YOU should be getting tea for me; I am sick, am I not?'

'Sorry, elder brother. And how could you be sick? It will be your enemies, if anyone has to, no?' He smiled broadly, and Rana smiled back, without feeling much like it.

'So..., no tea then. Anyway, I have something very important to tell you.' Obviously. Mohan always had. Important to him, at least. Rana waited for Mohan to continue.

'I saw someone today who should not be here.' The tone was matter of fact, but the face had an intense conviction drawn across. Rana felt uneasy, and tried to be derisive, though softening it at the last minute.

'Should not be here, hmmm. In what sense? Did you see a ghost? A foreigner? What exactly?'

'*Arrey* no! He just should not..., exist! Perhaps because I could not place him, nor put a label on him.' Rana made a mocking face at this, and Mohan tried to explain more.

'I mean, his caste, village, profession, even age – I could not make anything out. He was unreadable, whatstheword... Opaque!' He was obviously excited, but Rana still could not see the point.

'Mohan *pyare,* you have never been very good at reading people, so why bother this time?'

'No, no, this is different. It was as if this man has dropped out of the sky – with no signs of a past. And if you see him, you will notice it too.' And that joggled Rana's memory about his first waking thought a few minutes ago – about something having happened – is this what it was? Premonition of a visitor. But how could it be significant to him at all?

'I met Nalini too. She was asking about your health.' Mohan had moved back to his usual topics, and the look of seriousness was wiped off, again. 'And she is angry about something else - do you want to know about what?' Rana resigned himself, and pretended to listen, as Mohan droned on.

• • •

About three weeks later, before the end of November 1966, Rana was at the Indian Coffee House. Jehangirabad building, near the entrance to Hazratganj – with high arches and a walking corridor some steps above the street. He had come in that evening into the warm, smoky atmosphere, with people talking all around, and waiters in liveries maneuvering between tables. Rana liked it because it was somewhat like how he imagined Officers' Messes would be, though with more uniforms. He noticed Mohan waving his hand from across the hall and moved amidst the hubbub. Mohan was sitting with two others – one familiar, one not so. Rana stared hard at the profile of the latter but could not see any familiarity. And then he was at the table, and Mohan had gotten up, shook his hand, and proudly launched into introductions. This is Army Officer Ranveer Singh Rana. You know Professor Dikshit, and meet Shri Arjun Sharma, M.A. in Modern History from Allahabad University.

Rana brushed aside his own title with a curt 'not yet in the army, Mohan', shook hands with Dikshit ji, and turned towards the newcomer. The first thing he noticed was the look of wonder on the face; plain but unmarked, clear skin, healthy glow, a symmetric face. They shook hands, Sharma putting both his hands in it, a broad but nervous smile, and then a refined voice, 'Rana saheb. Have heard so much about you. Very nice to see you ag...., finally.' Rana noticed the respectful "*aap*" address, liked it, felt special, and overlooked the stutter. 'What kind of things?' He followed up the question with a smile. 'Good things, sir, only good things.' Sharma intoned, still pleasant, and oddly distracted.

Professor Dikshit interjected, coughing his own presence into this meeting, a possessive hand on Arjun Sharma's shoulder – 'meet our new History teacher. An incisive mind and a fresh perspective on history.' KK Dikshit was the Head of the History Department at the University, about fifty, with still dense, though greying, head of hair, his face beaming under the thick brown shell frames over his eyes, a loose bush-shirt covering his belly. Rana glanced again at Sharma, and found him staring back, as if he could not believe his eyes. And then it hit Rana, remembering Mohan's observation some days ago about the stranger he had seen that day. The word Mohan had used was "opaque", and looking at the man in front of him, Rana felt sure that Mohan had been talking about this specimen only. A mystery worth solving! They sat down, a coffee was ordered for Rana, and he tried to approach the topic diectly.

'New teacher? But where did you find him, Dikshit ji?' Rana looked around at Mohan, who was now gesturing towards Arjun Sharma with his eyes. Yes, yes, I know, Rana whispered and nodded at him. Meanwhile, Professor Dikshit was answering him.

'I did not have to. You know that we have been looking for a good teacher since Kapoor saheb left, and Sharma here came in with some strong credentials.' He beamed again at Sharma, clearly happy with his find.

'Finally! Hope his students also find him as good as you think he is.' Rana turned around and looked directly at Arjun, who now opened his mouth.

'Where do you live, Colonel..., I mean Rana saheb?' Rana frowned slightly, but answered the question, and Arjun nodded, as if getting a confirmation for something he already knew. Rana felt irritated for some reason, perhaps because he felt that this newcomer was trying to mock his career-aspiration, and decided to be rude.

'Okay..., Sharma ji, I am curious about something. How do modern historians decide what is important? For example, about the impact of this year's insufficient monsoon, or the death of Lal Bahadur Shastri under mysterious circumstances in Russia?'

Arjun Sharma was clearly surprised by the question, and for a moment Rana wondered whether he will even take the bait, but then Sharma started, 'you are right that it is not easy for contemporary historians. Their readers are citizens who are experiencing what is happening, and the historians themselves are citizens too. As a famous history teacher once said – the closer you get to the present, the more judgmental you become! And a good historian has to remain alert to this. That's the only way we can try to understand what is "more" important.' He stopped and looked around apologetically, and Rana, though unexpectedly satisfied with the answer, tried to contain himself from showing it.

The conversation continued, Mohan contributing with new topics – about recent student movements around the world and the news about protesting students in Delhi. All the while, Rana felt that he was being scrutinized – rather than the other way around – by the newcomer. Arjun Sharma was difficult to place, definitely. He appeared too young, well-fed and healthy to be a teacher, and his accent was neutral – no trace of any dominant Awadhi, Brij, or Purabiya dialect in it. Maybe he grew up elsewhere, but that information was never volunteered. They sat for some more time, and Rana later remembered the meeting especially because of being addressed as "Colonel". A simple joke, or something deeper?

• • •

Rana's CDSE test results came out in January. As expected he had qualified, and was called for the SSB Interview in March. Life appeared well set, and in about two years from now, he would get his commission in the Indian Army. Now, if he could only get the courage to share his dreams with Nalini.

But before that, just as 1967 started, Nalini already met the Opaque-man, thanks to Mohan again. Even in that first meeting (at the Zoo, of all places), where Rana was also present, he saw them with the red-tinted glasses of a jealous lover, and a suspicion raised its nasty head - that something is going to develop here; like some invisible electricity being transferred across and acknowledged. He was angry, but did not (or could not) find any specific cue to act, and had to tell himself that it is only his imagination. After all, he had his career and personal life to worry about. Even during the General Elections that happened in February, he was preoccupied with calculations of the heart. He did find it sinister though, that Arjun Sharma did not go to Allahabad to cast his vote. He himself went to Bareilly for a few days, and when he returned, he could not help but notice the pulling together of Nalini, Mohan and Arjun, and could even feel himself getting excluded from the group, their topics and interests taking them away on a slowly diverging trajectory.

A new government formed in Delhi in early March, Indira Gandhi became the PM again. Rana did not really think much about her, having a fuzzy resentment against nepotism; but he had heavier matters on his mind, and just as he about to give up, it happened. A meeting with Nalini at the Kwality restaurant, within the Mayfair theatre building in Hazratganj. He was leaving for his SSB interviews in a few days, and had slowly become convinced that if he waited till after the interview (and the inevitable selection) got over, Nalini would be spending more time with that Arjun, and who knows..., that he might really lose her. And so he hastened into this one-to-one meeting with Nalini.

Rana had ordered coffees and lemon puffs – fluffy and warm – for both of them, and thought that things were going well. Nalini wore a black kurta, long silver earrings hanging clear of her tightly tied hair, and he felt sure she had dressed up so well only for him. That impression remained only for the first few minutes. After that, as the silences deepened, he felt that Nalini was not meeting his eyes, nor could he find any cue or sign that would allow him to open his heart. Though he mumbled when he shared the "news" about his expected absence from Lucknow from June onwards, there was surety in his words, not allowing for any chance of him getting rejected by the Board. She made the right noises, and even smiled - when he spoke in a low, controlled tone - of his pride in joining the army. And then she continued, not with any notable passion but more matter of fact, and here it was.

'You (*aap*) are elder to me, and have been very good to..., to all of us; and I really, really want to wish you well in your chosen career, and..., in your life.' At this, he pounced, eager as a beggar on a thrown coin.

'But, Nalini, I do not want anyone else. I may not say much, but....', and he looked into her eyes. Where he saw - at first puzzlement, then realization, and then hesitation, followed shortly by modesty. Was she trying to avoid hurting him...?

'No..., what are you.... See, Ranveer, I did not think of you as.... Please do not think otherwise. Understand, please.'

It felt like he had run into a wall. His breath shortened, and he could only gape, both astounded and angry, while trying hard not to show it. He looked down at the crumbs on the plate, and picked up the coffee cup to drain it, but it was empty. Which is how his life felt, at that moment. Nalini took a sip from her cup, her eyes down and perhaps already preparing to leave. He thought of trying again, and even smiled to show acceptance, at least for now.

'Of course, I understand. But you must promise to write to me when I am in Dehradun. Or at least reply when I write a letter? Perhaps we just need to get to know each other better.' His smile froze in place, and did she respond with her own (artificial) smile?

He persisted, trying hard to make their meeting last, to keep her here longer on this shining glass-topped table. There were strands of her hair falling over the proud neck, next to the silver earrings, he did not want her to go yet, and desperately tried to think of questions to ask. Whether she wants to study more (yes, at least an M.A. degree), what subjects (Economics, perhaps, or History...), which city does she like more (Lucknow; also, Delhi, and alas she has not been to many places), and so on. The parting was awkward, but he persisted in escorting her to a rickshaw which she climbed for home. Rana could have gone along with her, and then on to his place from there, but he did not think she would like that. So he started walking the other way. With questions, anger and recriminations on his mind, but no solace to be found in any of them.

His mind remained troubled as the few days before his departure passed by, and he continued to suffer mentally - imagining all kind of things, including love blossoming between his Nalini and that intruder, Arjun Opaque Sharma!

Then he was on the train to Dehradun, and soon found himself in the middle of the official selection process, the psychology tests, interviews and the physicals.

And finally, at the end of it all, he failed to qualify! His physicals had gone well, but he remained distracted during the personal interview, and must have come across as blunt and somewhat cynical in the psychological tests – and they apparently did not want such personalities in the army.

Then, a slow, painful descent into the quagmire of middle-class struggle. Of largely his own making, admittedly. He could easily have gone back to Lucknow and landed some job. After all he had most of his contacts there. But he could not even consider going back. He turned it into a challenge for himself - to find a source of income, some work which could provide long-term security, to make things happen without using any of his previous acquaintances. With his degree, he could have easily gotten into teaching, but had never really considered that as a serious option. And it was not just the actual classroom teaching; even the thought now of spending time with young people, let alone being nice to them, felt abhorrent to him. He was sure of only one thing - that he cannot go back to Lucknow and show his face there! So, for the time being he shifted back to Bareilly, with his *mataji* at the old family house.

Finally, some kind of a breakthrough in August. His maternal uncle had set up business in Calcutta, in the trading of Jute. *Mataji* applied sisterly pressure, and her brother – Sarvesh *Mama* - invited him to join the business. Mama himself lived in Delhi, and moved between there and Calcutta, and occasionally Bareilly. Rana agreed, just to get away from the listless days passing excruciatingly by in his dear old small-town home. And so, the shift to the big city, the non-descript room in Jadavpur, and the tasteless office on Shakespeare Sarani. By the end of the year, he had settled in, at least at work, learning on the job – how to keep books, to handle customers and manage suppliers. And though he could not stop thinking about Nalini, he did not write to her.

• • •

In the beginning, every day was torture, dwelling on what could have been. Everything he had expected and assumed he was destined to have: a disciplined but privileged routine in army cantonments, starched uniforms, officers' club, and Nalini on his arm at dinners! But now? A resigned life in this big stinking city, with the smell of raw fish and stale water, and the lingering smoke of wood-fires on cold evenings? It was pitiful – so many people living on the streets – and getting used to that itself was a struggle. How to close your eyes to deprivation, and your heart to the inexorable guilt of having enough to eat and drink; it took some practice. The conditions in the big city kept getting worse, with lines of refugees trickling in from East Pakistan regularly.

He tried to distract himself, by taking train-rides outside. Digha beach, towards south, on the coast, was peaceful, and so was Shantiniketan to the north, and they were great antidotes to the big city. But it was not often, and most of the times, he would force himself into his work – such as it was – which kept him in the city; in the company of hard-headed businessmen or subservient (but canny) flunkeys. Not much intellectual stimulation, and rare company of the fairer sex, except a few at work. Along the way, he had decided against marriage, and did not give much opportunity to his mother to convince him otherwise. Slowly, she also gave up on that. *Mataji*, of course, stayed on in Bareilly, and preferred that he should visit her on festival times, at least. Which he tried. Mohan kept in touch, writing letters, and sharing the news. About people they had known together. Sometime in early 1968 Mohan wrote about Arjun and Nalini being together now, and that things were getting really serious – something Mohan had confirmed from one of her friends. Mohan seemed angry too for some reason, but Rana had no time for Mohan's anger – he was angry enough for himself.

Days, months, and then two years passed, as they have a habit of doing.

• • •

In early September 1969, a wedding card arrived in the post – "Nalini weds Arjun". That evening, Rana walked over to Hotel Darjeeling – not far from his office – and got drunk alone. He could have called a few people to join, but was in no mood for conversation. He had shaved off his moustache by now, and tried hard to stay in shape, forcing his life into a routine, and barely succeeding. After three pegs of whisky, sweat gathering on his brow – from the heat outside and the alcohol inside – his thoughts were turning angry, almost murderous. As he started on his fourth peg (last one! No more, he told himself), a song playing on the radio caught his attention – "*Jeevan se lambe hain, bandhu...*" – it sounded like Manna Dey, singing a melancholic, meditative songs, this one about the paths of life being longer even than life itself... Listening to the song, a memory was triggered – of Arjun singing this very song back in ... was it January or February 1967? It was definitely before Rana had gone for his SSB interview and failed that! He asked the waiter to increase the volume, and as he finished the last two fingers of his drink in slow sips, he shuddered, and remembered that "performance".

That day, they had been meeting within the Lucknow University campus, where Arjun was already settling down very well, the "Opaque-man" finding friends and followers (too) easily! Sitting on chairs and sipping tea, teachers (a few younger ones), students, and Rana as a special invitee (and he, in turn, deciding to feel like an outsider). He could not help but notice how Arjun stood out even in that crowd. The knowing smile, disarming handsomeness and refined words. In between, Mohan had happened to mention that the new professor also sings. Words of encouragement all round, and then Arjun had sung a few lines of this song, after mentioning that it was written by a new poet - none of them would have heard of him. He was not even sure which film it was taken from, but it did not matter. Everyone was spellbound by the pathos of the words and the clear voice, and Rana noticed the look on Nalini's face. He had tried even after that, at the Kwality restaurant, but...

In Calcutta, the song finished on the Radio, and as Rana hungrily gulped some water, he heard the voice announcing the name of the just released film it was from, sung by Manna Dey, and written by Gulzar. Was that the name Arjun had mentioned – Rana thought so. But how could the "Opaque-man" have known the song more than two years ago? Rana's head started throbbing. Opaque, "*Dhundhla*" is what the man really is – partly visible, unclear, and impenetrable. And my Nalini (yes, still mine!) is marrying this "Opacity"! He was shaking his head now. There is no other way but to take some strong action. Something, anything, to try to stop this, this...ceremony, from happening. He took out the ugly-looking wedding card from his folder and opened it. A civil ceremony, apparently, because there was no description of any rituals being planned, only a dinner the same evening at the Carlton. On September 14, 1969. He had to go to Lucknow, as soon as possible.

Next morning: Reconsideration. The convictions of night-time melted away easily in the bright sunlight, more so perhaps because those convictions had been fueled by alcohol. What could he really do - now that they have decided to marry each other? If he confronts Sharma with the kind of questions he had on his mind, they would surely think of him as insane. So, what was to be done? Though he could not bear the thought of going to Lucknow for the wedding, he could not miss it either, could he?

In the end, he decided to travel anyway. Otherwise he would never know, he thought. He resolved to stay away from the actual gathering, but would meet Mohan (definitely), and Arjun (if possible), and would just have to console himself by observing Nalini from afar. Watch her. And desire her. Things nobody could take away from him.

• • •

Tuesday, September 9, 1969. Rana caught the newly started Rajdhani Express from Howrah, paying Rs 90 for a superfast AC Chair Car travel done in less than 18 hours! Lucknow was nice and quiet after the hubbub of Calcutta. And just like that, his eyes almost welled up with tears as the rickshaw moved past the University road, on the way to a lodge in Daliganj. "Just a bloody civilian" – that's what he had become. The bitterness refused to leave him, and familiar sights only made it worse!

Mohan met him in the afternoon, physically the same but somewhat more serious-faced than Rana remembered. Mohan shared the news that he was shifting to Delhi soon, thanks to a job in the Railways. They talked about many other things, but not about Nalini directly. Mohan rambled on, nervous, about how the wedding date had to be planned based on Pitra-Paksha, which was starting on the 25th. Etcetera. Mohan also arranged for him to meet Arjun that evening. Kindly declining to join them. At the Coffee House.

That evening, when they met, Arjun appeared confused and surprisingly apologetic, treating Rana like an elder. This was unexpected, and Rana could not get himself to express the anger he had been nursing all this while. Arjun was also smoking, and seemed to have lost some of his healthy glow. None of my business, Rana thought, and congratulated him briefly, but was almost waved off by Arjun. And then...

'I have to tell you, Rana sa'b, that I had not planned for any of this to happen. I came here... for something else entirely!'

'Good to hear. And what was it that you came here for?' Rana had to ask, his bitterness about Nalini bubbling over. The answer was voiced slowly, coming in between drags of smoke.

'Even if I tell you, you will not believe. All I can say is that I did complete the work I came for. It is just that..., that I realized that I cannot go back! And now I am also trying to complete this bloody research and my PhD.' Arjun grimaced, and there was sadness in his eyes. What is he sad about, Rana wondered? And thought if he should ask about that Manna Dey song. Decided against it, but still, he had to say this.

'You are not making sense, Sharma, and you know it. You also know that we have nothing to talk about, and so I will not take your time. I had thought of asking some other things – like where have you really come from - but I am not sure if that will change anything. The only thing I want to say very clearly to you is this: If, because of you, Nalini gets into any kind of trouble, I will do whatever I can to make your life miserable. My life is already... set on its own path, but I will not allow her to face any..., any suffering from your hands!' He stopped and got up, not wanting to be there anymore.

'Rana sa'b, I assure you of that, and the only thing I would also say is..., to not lose hope. Who knows...?"

Arjun got up as well, they shook hands, Rana eager to leave, and Arjun persistent, as if still trying to make him understand. Rana left, wondering about the mystery – which seemed to have become even deeper. But he was tired - of this life, of people, especially people who cannot be yours to hold. The long days ahead in the god-forsaken Metropolis of Calcutta were nothing to look forward to – but at least it was a known evil. Here, he could not understand anyone anymore.

Before that, he had one more task to complete, and so back to the lodge and then a drink or two at the nearby bar. In the morning, unshaven and haggard (but it did not matter), he met Mohan and requested him for one last favor. They worked out the final plan before he left for Calcutta. He had to wait out two agonizing, boring, stretched-out days for that.

• • •

It was a Friday, two days before the wedding, Rana was still hanging around in Lucknow, and a picnic had been planned by some of Nalini's friends from the university. At the Residency. Based on Mohan's information, Rana reached there in advance. Bright morning among the ruins of the medieval architecture, pock-marked with cannon-ball shaped holes in the walls here and there, set against green lawns and trees laid out over the expanse of the monument. He found a spot inside from where the entrance was clearly visible, and waited, nervously tapping his feet, and cursing under his breath.

Finally, closer to noon time: a group of women entered, their voices carrying over the distance, and he caught sight of her over the distance and across the ruins. He got up and moved behind a wall, leaning against the thin-brick structure, and watched. Nalini wore a loose salwar-suit, green, paired with a lemon dupatta, her hair untied & shorter than he remembered, her eyes hidden behind a pair of large sunglasses. He gazed hungrily, trying to decipher any sign of dejection, or even of a lack-of-enthusiasm, in her visage, her posture. But she appeared carefree, perhaps even happy, as the group of women walked inside the monument, swinging bags and a couple of baskets (food for the picnic?). He crept along, hiding behind walls and trees, wherever he could, shamefaced but determined. Till they settled themselves down on the main lawn near an old cannon, in the shade of a tree. There was no way for him to get any closer now, and as he turned his face away in anger (mixed with what felt like shame), he heard snatches of a song – they were singing! He narrowed and focused his eyes on the green-clothed woman across the expanse of the lawn, saw her take her sunglasses off, and laugh happily, her head thrown back.

He left the Residency chastened and totally dejected. And left Lucknow that night. Time to go back and resume his life in Calcutta.

To his credit (or his stubbornness) he felt incapable of thinking of marriage. There are sorrows other than love..., as they say. But for him, that seemed to be the only one right now.

[When you are in the rush of living, you just live (Rana thinks now); forks appear on roads and you take one, and so it goes on. You rarely bother about the paths not travelled. Most of the time. And after the disappointment with Nalini and then with SSB, those Calcutta years did pass by like that. Perhaps he should have examined his decision (his blindness?) more closely. Because its only when you turn your head and start looking back that the forks become visible. But, if he had taken any of the other forks then – like giving in to his mother and getting into an arranged marriage – how would he have found the later happiness? The joy that was to dawn on him in abundance...?]

CHAPTER VII

1977-1987

26 November 1977. Rana can never forget the day he got the news. Over the last eight years, he had stayed on in Calcutta, moving into a larger house near Alipore, had saved some money by now, and kept the focus on his work, his occasional visits to Sonagachi, and his book collection. He had regrown his moustache and was keeping his hair long – more so from laziness than to make a fashion statement, though. He was still in good health, without having to work extra hard for it. As the decade passed by, Mohan got married (Rana did not attend), Pakistan got split in two, and Indira Gandhi became a veritable goddess. Not for long though. Unrest bubbled over, till the country first burnt and then went very quiet – under the national Emergency that was announced in 1975. Then, after almost two years, Mrs. Gandhi lifted the Emergency, and announced elections, which she promptly lost. Since earlier this year, there was a new Prime Minister in the country – the first PM to head a non-Congress government - and a lot of things seemed to have changed. It was as if the country grew up overnight. Not much had changed for Rana though, except he had grown older, picked up some Bangla language, and saved some money. Nalini was like a pleasant dream he had once had.

Anyway, that day he was in his office (still on Shakespeare Sarani – though bigger now), and going through some files, when he heard the phone ring on the front desk. He waited, and heard some sounds – the inevitable hello, and then the mumbled voices, and then a “please hold”. After a moment, Mrs. D’Souza knocked on his door and came in – ‘you have a trunk call from Delhi.’ Most days, she seemed disapproving, though not so much now; there was actual concern in her voice.

He went over and picked up the phone, ‘hello, Rana here.’ First there was the static and then a voice from afar – ‘Rana Bhai, sorry, but I have some bad news.’ He recognized the voice of Mohan. What the hell, he wondered, and started asking what had happened. But Mohan was already talking, almost shouting – ‘... died yesterday in a train accident. Yes, Arjun Sharma, passed away! You know what I mean? Nalini........’ there was disturbance in between, and he himself shouted, ‘what?’ and then the final words, ‘...shattered! The poor widow!’

Putting down the phone, he stood next to it for a while – gazing into nothingness – till Mrs. D’Souza came back and looked at him with curiosity and concern. He told her briefly that someone close to him has passed away, and he would have to go out of station for a few days, and she said ok, let me know if a train ticket has to be booked. And he instructed her, said thanks, and coming back to the cabin in a daze, fell into his chair. He stared at the ceiling, his mind in a whirl. Nalini as a widow – white sari, etc.? And he remembered what Arjun Sharma had told him in their last meeting – that he should not lose hope. But does that make sense at all? Dare he hope? Would she?

The following week, he was in Lucknow. Mohan also came – accompanied by his wife and a toddler son - and there were other people too; friends that the Sharma’s must have made after marriage, some relatives from Nalini’s side, none from Arjun Sharma’s side, and Rana felt out of place, out of his depths. How do you really console someone at their husband’s death? Every time he saw Nalini, he saw the cruelty of the situation playing out across her face. The worst was that there was no body for cremation. Dr. Sharma had gone to Ahmedabad for some work, and while travelling back, the mail train he was traveling in, was derailed by suspected terrorists in Haryana near Rewari station, with two coaches completely destroyed. Arjun's name was among the people who died in that accident, but some bodies could not even be identified.

Even in that somber atmosphere, he could not help his memories, and along with them, the old desires, awakening – and he found it difficult to be near her. Initially, he wanted to wait till Nalini would be by herself, and by the time he made up his mind to visit, he found that her sister was still living with her, supporting Nalini in her hour of grief. So, he made up some vague consoling noises and left soon. He realized that Nalini would need more time before, before... anything.

He decided to visit Bareilly for a few days, mainly to spend time with his mother, who was not keeping well. Sarvesh *mama* had also come from Calcutta, so Rana hinted to them that he may not go back to the trading office in Calcutta; that things have changed. He was old enough now that both the elders in his life could not order him anymore. It was a pleasant holiday, ultimately, and at the time of departure, when his dear *Mataji* told him to "get married, beta", he took it as a good omen (she had told him that after years), and said that he would try.

• • •

Back in Lucknow, early December of the same year, he went to Sharma's flat in Badshah Bagh, within the University campus. Nalini was retaining the same flat – she was a lecturer now anyway. It was a Sunday evening

– around teatime. She was wearing a white sari, covered with a black woolen shawl, her hair open, short, a stony expression on her face. Rana tried to stay calm, and made light conversation about his mother, and about Calcutta. Nalini, in response, was mostly non-verbal, but opened up slowly.

'I think he knew he was not coming back.' Rana only raised his eyebrows in a question, and she continued.

'When he was leaving for Ahmedabad on 17 November – he was going for a meeting at Gujarat University about some manuscripts - that morning, we were sitting and talking in this room only. Like we are sitting now. He said that if something happens to him, I should not give up on life. And..., then that railway telegram...!' Her eyes were wet, and she hung her head down for a minute. Rana waited; he could not think of anything to say.

'I don't understand why they could not send his b...., him, home. At least we would have seen him, done the last rites. This way, I cannot even cry properly.' She grimaced, as if in pain, and looked at him. Rana tried to pick his words carefully.

'I know. It is not easy. Just do not forget that there are people who care for you. Your family, friends....' In response, Nalini started a rambling monologue.

'We had our 8th anniversary recently when we went for dinner at our special place. And I have no hesitation in saying this, that he never gave me any reason to complain. Any big reason, I mean. He had his own tensions, even demons – I think - but he did not take out anything on me. There were parts of his life that were like a mystery, yes. About this trip also - why did he not take a direct train back to Lucknow? Also, about two years ago, he had gone to Banaras for a few days – saying that he had to meet some relatives there. And when he came back, for a long time, it was as if he was haunted – by something.'

Rana stayed quiet, and let her ramble. So, the man was opaque even at home? Finally, she got up and went inside. Rana picked up the Pioneer newspaper and tried to read. After a few minutes she came back out, face washed, hair tied in a loose bun, and two cups of tea on a small steel tray. With the tea, she opened up again.

'You know, they only found his purse, with the train ticket, the University card, our address, a phone number - of Prof Kumar, P/P my name - a photo and some money, and .... The photo was mine.' Her head was down, and her shoulders shook slightly. He stopped himself from touching her, and she controlled herself after a few seconds.

'I have never said this to any of my family. But it IS different with you – you had known Arjun from before. Did you ever notice anything? Anything like..., like premonitions?' Just thinking about this had perked her up, and Rana decided to bring up that Manna Dey song.

'Do you remember that day in early 1967? We were sitting in the university campus – in the forecourt of the History building? And Arjun had sung this song about the long pathways of life. You remember?' In response, she smiled, looking into her teacup.

'Yes. And later also, I always enjoyed listening to his poetry – never his own, as he said – but they were good. I have no idea where he used to get it from, but he recited them well. Sometimes he would sing.'

'That's what I am saying. That song, it is from a movie that released in 1969.' She nodded absently, and he felt that she had not really grasped his point.

'You know, just a few days ago he was telling me that the Janata Party will break up soon, and that Indira Gandhi will become the PM again by 1980!' She was smiling inwardly, perhaps thinking about Arjun speaking out his prophecies.

'You do not need any special premonition about that – the whole country is watching. Let us see if his predictions come true.' Rana smiled – for the first time since his arrival. She smiled too, but not at him; she was still lost in remembrance.

'He was different.' She finally intoned and seemed to come back to the present. Rana agreed totally with that observation, but did not say anything, and she continued, with an effort – 'but okay. Tell me about yourself. How is life in Calcutta?'

Relieved, Rana shared parts of his life again, telling her that he is thinking of shifting back to Bareilly, that his mother's health is deteriorating, and he has had enough of Calcutta for now. He was actually ready to conclude this visit. She was still so desirable to him, and he was desperately trying to end his bachelorhood, finally. That actually made it difficult to sit and watch her. It was unclear to him though as to what she was thinking. Whether she wanted him to leave or not? Then she looked up, and (perhaps) realized that he was ready to go. He got up slowly, trying to smile – but then his mouth twisted, ruing the inevitability of loss – and their eyes met, a stretched moment longer than he had expected. And she turned her gaze sideways and upwards, as if remembering other times. Still looking away, she spoke.

'It was good you came.' And then, after a pause as he waved his right hand in a "leave it" gesture, she continued, head almost turned away - 'Long hair does not suit you that much.'

• • •

The next time Rana visited Nalini was about five months later. Meanwhile, he wrapped up his affairs in Calcutta – with some token disappointment shown by Sarvesh *Mama*, but practically no regrets of his own – and had already started searching for a possible job or a contract in Lucknow. Mataji was stable, though fragile from her weak heart, and he tried to be the caring son. In May 1978, he had to come to Lucknow to meet an IAS officer on Rana Pratap Marg. And after the meeting - without any favorable conclusion, but another brick in the wall, hopefully - he went to Nalini's flat in Badshah Bagh.

Late afternoon, glaring heat in the mid-May air, made somewhat tolerable by the trees around the building. Knocking at her door, he hoped she was at home. After a wait, her voice – 'who is there?' He replied with his name and could only imagine her reaction at this persistent voice from the past. Then the door opened partly, her face appeared, and, '*Aap*? Sorry, I was just getting ready. Two minutes?' And he, very accommodative, and ready to wait outside. The door closed after a half-smile from her, and he turned around to walk over to the look-out at the end of the corridor on this 3rd floor.

Quicker than he had anticipated, she reopened the door and invited him in. Cream-colored salwar-kurta, with an understated golden-bordered dupatta, hair tied up, and her long fingers passing him a glass of water. She looked young, again, and to Rana's eyes, a vision. The fan was moving nicely, her room was high-ceilinged, cool and pleasant, with a whiff of talcum powder in the air, though he could not see any visible trace on her. She enquired about him, agreeing with his shift from Calcutta to Bareilly, and did not make any direct reference to his hair – which he was wearing shorter again. He asked her about how she is managing, and she was animated in response about the classes she will start teaching once the new session starts. And that she did not want to stay with her parents, though she was meeting them frequently, at their new house in Paper Mill Colony. The Chand Ganj house was very old, and better off locked, if not sold. They talked about other friends from before, including Mohan – now in Delhi, and the proud father of a five-year old son. And then she picked up a photo from the mantelpiece – a studio picture of Arjun and hers. Black & white, with only her sari colored pink. Sitting side by side, Arjun staring in the distance in a (white?) half-sleeved shirt, handsome as ever, to Rana's still-jealous eyes, and Nalini, beautiful, proud, looking satisfied with life. Looking at the photo, she turned serious again.

'I will not forget Arjun. Just because I am smiling and trying to live my life again, does not mean that I have forgotten my marriage. He was – and you had known him too – special, and never gave me any trouble. Except one.' Rana nodded his head in encouragement and took the photo frame from her hand to look at it. She continued, more hesitant now, 'for some reason, he did not want to become a father. I don't know, but there was something...' Rana kept nodding in sympathetic understanding. The shadow of the *Dhundhla aadmi* - Opaque-man - was still around.

They continued talking for some more time, she cut some mangoes to eat, and he felt comfortable with her. Perhaps for the first time, there was no need to make an effort to appear good or smart or attractive. Just an acceptance of the way things are. Finally, as he got up to leave, and she came to the door with him, smiling and looking desirable as ever, he dared himself. Circling her shoulder with his hand, and pulling her slightly closer, he told her, 'keep smiling, always.' She stayed that way, her eyes down, till he let go of her, and waving goodbye, left.

Walking down the stairs, his hand tingled where he had touched her skin, and he kept it in his pocket, savoring the memory.

• • •

Finally, the day came. The day he had waited for, imagined, even fantasized about for long years. And a day that was easy to remember – Independence day 1979 – at the Lucknow University canteen next to the newly built Ladies' Hostel. Nalini was dressed in a sari again, worn for efficiency, draped with expertise. Her face flushed (like old times) and reflected the pink of her blouse beautifully. She had only said, "I think I am ready,' and smiled, and he had felt so happy (and bold), that he covered her hand on the table with his own. Finally. Independence Day had brought about its own kind of freedom for him.

This moment had come after months of patience, of waiting, hoping and planning. He had managed to get a supply contract from the UP Cooperative Federation in Lucknow before the end of 1978, took a house for rent in Mahanagar, and even convinced his mother to come and stay with him for some time. Though Mataji had not liked it at first, Lucknow grew on her, her health stabilized, and she settled herself into the routine of being a relaxed matriarch at home; sitting in the front portico on most days and watching the convent school ground just across the road from their house – where boys in uniform would play and parade under the watchful eyes of white-robed Catholic priests and various PT teachers.

Now, Nalini was talking about her visit to Gujarat for a field trip; they were doing research on the economic impact of natural disasters, and the recent floods in Rajkot were a good case study of that – thousands of people dead, one complete town and many villages destroyed. He initially felt, and expressed it too - that there was something wrong with a tragedy being a source of excitement and exploration for academicians, but she was appropriately somber about the destruction itself. He could only look at her in amazement, and bask in the sunshine of his good fortune.

Her admission of readiness on that Independence Day was a delayed response to a letter he had written to her a few weeks ago, in which he had asked her to take her time, and that he will wait till she is ready. And then he had added – half in humor – that he hoped she would finally be "ready" before he turns senile.

And now, on this National holiday, patriotic songs playing on some loudspeaker nearby, and their fingers touching, he talked about being together and making a life in Lucknow – where it had all begun. Of course, amidst this culmination of his decade-old dream, the only thing hanging like a cloud was the memory of Arjun. At this moment though, he felt confident he would be able to make it go away, by giving her a new life and a proper family – including a child, hopefully. But first, the critical interview with *Mataji*.

• • •

Mataji sat on the diwan, a shawl over her knees, her white sari covering the head. She had her prayer beads in her right hand, her left palm resting in her lap. The shoulders were still mostly straight and proud, the slight drooping caused perhaps also by the fact of having an unmarried middle-aged son at home. Nalini wore a light blue sari, the blouse solemnly white. The only thing covering her head were a pair of sunglasses, and her confidence was clearly visible. Confidence that came not just from having seen the world, but also from surviving robustly. Rana felt proud of her, though trying not to show it too much.

They were in the front porch of his house in Mahanagar on this Saturday afternoon. The didonia hedge was still not fully grown, and you could see across the road, directly into the large school ground, where a football game was going on. The ground was circled by rows of wires – thick iron and spikes. A few years later, they would build a wall around the ground, so you could not see anything inside. But that was later.

Mataji stayed quiet after the initial greetings, and they sat down – Rana on a cotton-padded stool made of bamboo, Nalini on the edge of the diwan. She perched lightly, her shoulders covered by her sari, her lips bowed slightly in an easy smile. Mataji was perceptive, immediately realizing that she was not interviewing the usual, every-day, *bahu*-to-be. She looked at their faces – the woman, mature but with "*paani*" – a liquid glow - still in her face, and her only son, who had clearly (finally, sigh...) chosen to marry. She closed her eyes for a few seconds, while Rana and Nalini glanced at each other, eyes locked, smiles fleeting quickly across, like shadows on walls. And then Mataji opened her eyes, and spread her hands forward, first as a blessing, and then as on offer to hold. And when they offered their own, she held them with tight anxiety. 'Be happy', she said, her words hurried, but then she smiled, and Nalini bowed her head in a respectful thanks.

A few minutes later, Pooran brought in tea and biscuits, and they sipped and tried to make conversation. While watching the football game in the school ground. Mataji asked about her parents, and Nalini answered, but with a visible lack of enthusiasm. 'Chachaji is not very happy, but he was not very happy ten years ago either, so....' Nalini used to address her father as "Chachaji" for some reason. But, 'Chachi understands.' She smiled at Mataji to show that she was not bitter about it. Because, 'luck has not favored me so far, *bas*!' Although, 'days are changing, I can feel that.' She had a determined look about her when she said that, as if confidence would help in turning her luck.

In the school ground across the street, something was happening. About a dozen boys had formed a circle, and one adult, obviously the instructor, was just inside the circle. They could not see what was transpiring inside that huddle of students. People had stopped to watch from the road also. And then sounds travelled across the ground – of something sharply cutting through the air. One could only imagine punishment being meted out to an errant student.

Mataji sighed loudly and spoke to Rana next, as if conveying that Nalini did not need any instructions from her. 'Congratulations, *beta*. Your penance of years had finally been blessed. Take good care of her now.'

But then, she remembered, and addressed Nalini, 'but, *beti*, you people are brahmins, no? Your mother and father..., will they not have any problems because of that?'

Nalini was thoughtful, 'Ma ji (may I call you that...); even if they once worried about those things, I do not think they would bother. After all, their "widowed" daughter is getting another chance.'

She never really stopped to hear Mataji's assent to her half-question, and now turned around to look at Rana, '...and please do not start worrying that I am thinking like that; I am only stating "their" point-of-view.' And when Rana stayed stone-like, 'really! I am not feeling "sorry" for myself.' Smile, reciprocated, mutual nods of heads.

Mataji gave up her remaining struggle then. After years of seeing her son without a life-partner, she had no prior experience of facing a prospective *bahu* like this. And her first reaction - when Rana had told her that he was bringing a lady to meet her – was panic. Panic at losing her son to a woman. Yes, it was getting late in life for him, but why a widow? So, she had tried to harden herself before the meeting. No more, now: the woman seemed capable, and at least she was not bringing a child with her. She sighed with relief; time to let someone else take care of her beloved son. And perhaps now she will get to see a grandson before passing on.

After dinner that night, as they were sitting together, Rana reading the newspaper again, and drinking hot milk in a steel tumbler, Mataji observed – 'She is good, but... a little dark, no?' In her mind, pointing out a flaw was a sure way to avoid the evil eye.

• • •

Rana paid a return visit to meet Nalini's parents; at their first-floor flat in Paper Mill Colony. There was a large terrace outside, but he did not get to enjoy the terrace, because they sat in the tube-lighted drawing room instead. There were wooden chairs with cotton-stuffed cushions on them, a sun-mica covered center table, a frame-mounted poster of ducks on the wall, and a cupboard with knick-knacks and some books. Shukla ji (his future father-in-law!) joined them for some time, answering his greetings shortly, sitting quietly, as the conversation failed to gather steam, and then getting up to go inside. Chachi waved that off as a problem, explaining that it was time for his evening prayer, anyway. She was fatalistic, 'now *beta*, what can we say, if you people have already decided? Only (she folded her hands), take care of my daughter. She has suffered...' Rana tried to convey, through gestures and short sentences, that she need not worry about that and noticed from the corner of his eyes that Nalini looked amused. Then Chachi was asking about his parents, and Rana asked her to consider coming and meeting his mother. It was just a formality now.

• • •

They got married in early 1980. Indira Gandhi had already become Prime Minister of the country once again – proving Arjun right - but Rana was not worrying about it anymore, feeling sure they were over that hangover by now.

After the thankfully-brief Arya-Samaj rituals at her house in Paper Mill Colony, they had planned a dinner at his house in Mahanagar. Nalini had offered to share the expenses, but he convinced her that he was perfectly capable of handling that. Thanks to his savings of the last decade of bachelorhood, and the financially rewarding state government contracts he was already starting to acquire.

For the occasion that evening, Rana dressed up better than he had ever before. Including a silk kurta with a Kashmir shawl over it, and Rajasthani jootis on his feet! All selected by Nalini. Nothing to be ashamed of, she told him, it's your wedding after all. And the bride, in a gold-embroidered sari, with a rose in her hair, and a smile which seemed frozen on her face throughout the evening.

There were about two dozen people at dinner, including the hosts and his in-laws. Mohan had come from Delhi, accompanied by his wife and son. He had put on weight and lost some hair, but retained the innocent enthusiasm of old – perhaps because of the occasion. His wife, overdressed, overly made-up, but not speaking much. And their son,

Ravi Mishra, 7 years young, with inherited good-looks, but unbearably spoilt. They ate together, and Nalini and Mohan kept recalling good memories from their student days, Mrs. Mishra tried hard to retain interest, while Rana looked on indulgently, happy with life.

After the dinner was over, and those guests who had to leave had left, Nalini moved away to help *Mataji* handle other arrangements. Rana and Mohan wandered out together, towards the *paan* stall a few meters away at the Gole Market *Chauraha*. Rana asked for a *meetha paan*, and Mohan, after lighting a cigarette, started speaking.

'Elder brother, congratulations again.' Rana, with an easy smile tipped his hand in a salute. Mohan continued, smoke coming out in intermittent puffs as he spoke, reminiscently.

'I cannot help but remember Sharma – my guruji! You remember that day? When he had dropped into our lives? It was perhaps 14-15 years ago?' Rana stiffened, involuntarily, and looked around, as Mohan continued.

'It was tragic, his death! But if he had not died.....' As Mohan wondered, Rana turned his eyes away from the obvious but discomforting conjecture, and towards the road.

The *Chauraha* had one road coming from his house, and going towards Faizabad road, and another coming from Nishatganj and heading to Wireless, Dandaiya and other localities beyond. There was a rickshaw parked on the Wireless side of the road, and Rana's eyes made out the shape of a man sitting in it, and even in the dark it looked as if the man had turned around and was looking towards them. Rana stared hard, and took a step forward. Then he saw the man tap the rickshaw-wala on his back, and they started out in the distance, moving away. Rana shivered, and turned around – time to go back. Shaking his head, he placed a brotherly arm around Mohan's shoulder, and they walked back.

• • •

Ranjini was born in mid-1981 at the Fatima Hospital. Nalini was now 33, but the pregnancy went better than expected, at least according to the doctor. Rana had started questioning the whole idea by the end of it, as he listened to her cries of pain from outside the room. But it was okay in the end; in a few days they were back at their Mahanagar home, and except for some initial health problems, Ranju – as they started calling her - grew up with a combination of unalloyed love and discipline that her parents improvised upon, in their own journey of parenthood.

The next time the memory of Arjun Sharma intruded upon them was when Rana & Nalini went to watch the Hindi comedy film - Angoor. Nalini liked certain kind of movies, and though Rana did not share her taste completely, he would accompany her to support and participate in her enthusiasms. After the movie, once they were back at home for their evening tea, and Ranjini was safely ensconced in her mother's lap, that Nalini brought up the topic. She had really enjoyed the comedy, laughing at times even when Rana did not find anything funny. Now, she started talking about Arjun.

'Do you know; Arjun would have really liked this movie? He used to say this about Gulzar, that he really has a rhythm in his direction, and a picture in his mind about how a scene should flow. He would have loved Gulzar's first real attempt at comedy.' She was smiling wistfully, as she lifted the baby up in the air, and Ranju laughed back at her.

Rana was not sure what to say, and could only smile in response. In his mind, he was only wishing that her Arjun-hangover went away finally. And he felt sure that Ranju's presence would help in this.

When the Indian cricket team won the World Cup in June 1983, Nalini was eagerly cheering them along, while listening to the radio commentary in the evening, as the game concluded in England. Rana would marvel at her interest in the sports, but had no hesitation in buying a Videocon TV later that month, so that they could watch Chitrahaar and the Sunday-evening films sitting at home.

Next year, they were all shocked by the news about Indira Gandhi's assassination by her own bodyguards on the last day of October, but the riots that followed were even worse. For a few days, the country seemed like it was going to the dogs again, with the horrors of partition revisited, except this time, it was mostly Congress Party goons who attacked sikh citizens of the country! The PM's son succeeded her, of course, in the best traditions of Indian dynastic democracy! Rajeev Gandhi was the erstwhile pilot who had recently joined politics at the emotional time of his brother's plane accident, and now took over the prime ministership under even more tragic circumstances! And then the general elections again, which saw the Congress party getting its largest majority ever, and so the young PM was anointed by the citizens also.

In 1987, Ranju got admission at Mount Carmel School, less than a kilometer away. Rana would walk her to school and Nalini would bring her back. Life was good for him again. He was getting new contracts, thanks to his cultivation of a favorable new commercial officer – Raj Kumar Gupta - at the PCF office. This time - for supplying jute bags for all of their fertilizer purchases. Nalini was happy and growing in her teaching career, and their love retained its spiciness. Was it thanks to the late marriage, or something else; he could never be certain of that. But he was not one to complain about good fortune.

[And this good fortune (Rana thinks again) – would it have been his, if he had taken any of the other forks that came earlier in his path? And that's the eerie part! The diary he has just read is talking about a completely different path altogether. Marrying Nalini was a dream, and it came true. Being a father was another, and he could do that too. But then... was 1967 a turning point in life? Every choice actually is, isn't it?]

CHAPTER VIII

1991-2001

In was in 1991, at the *Griha Pravesh* of their new house in B-Block, Indira Nagar, that Rana first noticed young Ravi Mishra. Mohan and his son had come from Delhi for the occasion. They were sitting down in the portico of the house, in the shade, and there was a table fan directed at them. The rituals and the lunch were over, and the smell of fresh paint, mixed with flowers and food was all around. Sitting with them was Raj Kumar Gupta, now a General Manager at the UP PCF office, and Rana's main liaison there. Gupta - dark, grey-haired, humble looking but sharp - had become a close family friend of Rana. Also Mohan, comfortably fat now, dressed in white kurta, a lighted cigarette in his hand. And Rana himself, also in white, clean-shaven, receding and greying hair, eyeglasses, but still trim, feeling satisfied with life. Except for the regret that his Mataji could not live to see this occasion. But at least she had the chance to enjoy her granddaughter for a few years - Rana told himself, and came back to the present. Mohan had turned to his son and was asking Rana to bless him.

– 'this useless guy got admission at the Engineering College in Lucknow. Can you imagine? My beta will be an Engineer!' Mohan was practically gloating, though trying to hide it behind humor. Rana congratulated the boy, who did not look too obnoxious considering his age. Blue jeans and kurta, clean-cut face, well-kept hair, composed face. Ravi had touched his feet with a sincere expression, and that had really impressed Rana. Mohan was still talking. About the impending order for implementation of Mandal

Commission in colleges, and how lucky Ravi was to have gotten admission this year. Who knows what will happen to the general category students next year?

Gupta decided to take his leave, and Rana went with him till the gate to bid goodbye and thank him for coming; and they folded hands at each other. When he came back to sit, Rana noticed that Ranjini had already joined them, and was chatting with her Mohan uncle. A piece of her father's heart – her face a fortunate combination of her parents' best features, and curious and friendly by nature. Nalini also came out behind her daughter, as most of the other guests were now gone, even her parents. They chatted. The most burning topic, of course, was the bomb explosion in May, which had killed Rajiv Gandhi and many others in Tamil Nadu, and investigations were still going on about how this was done, who was to blame, etc. Rana and family had watched the state funeral on their new Color TV! Then Mohan changed the subject, and asked Ranju about her school. She praised the school, but also grumbled about having to travel so far to Mahanagar. Then she turned towards her father and complained (once more) that she had liked the house there, that Indira Nagar was not as nice. Rana consoled her, and as he said "sorry" to his daughter, he caught Nalini's eye. She rolled them, and mumbled the words (a frequent occurrence) – 'go on, spoil your princess!'

As he looked around, Rana noticed that Ravi was mostly quiet, not talking much, and appearing to be there only as a duty. Mohan and Ravi left soon afterwards, heading towards Sitapur Road where the Institute was - to check the hostel and other campus facilities. The session would start from the next month, and he would be coming then with bag and baggage. Being nominated the local guardian for the boy, Rana knew that they would be seeing more of him in the coming years.

• • •

hich they did soon. Ravi had joined the Institute in late August, and in mid-October, just a few weeks into the new session, he landed on their doorstep in Indira Nagar with a bag on his back. It seems that they got two extra days off for Vijayadashmi, and he had just felt like going home, and so he came, hoping that 'uncle' would help him get to Delhi somehow. Rana felt that there was more to the story than that, perhaps a desire to escape from ragging? Understandable, but he later came to be sure that that one day was the starting point, a trigger, for Ranjini to get to know her Ravi bhaiya, and thus start the turning of a cruel cycle.

Rana had some audit in the office that day, and left home after breakfast, along with Nalini. Like they always did – earlier on his motorcycle, but since a few months now - in their new Maruti 800 car. He would typically drop Nalini at the University in the morning. On the way back, if he were coming early, he would pick her up, otherwise she would take a rickshaw back home. Ranjini had already left for school earlier. They instructed Pooran to take care of Ravi, and so it happened that when Ranjini reached home that afternoon, there was nobody else at home. Except Pooran, of course, but he was getting old, and would generally rest in the afternoons after serving the girl her lunch.

Anyway, when Rana came home in the evening, he was told that Ravi had gone with Ranjini and another friend of hers to the nearby Lekhraj Market. For ice-creams, it seems. While sitting down for tea with Nalini, though they talked of this and that, his mind was stuck in Lekhraj Market.

Nalini was nonchalant, and even had a few words of praise for Mohan's boy. Rana told her that he had talked to Mohan, and has managed to book a ticket for Ravi on Gomti Express for next morning. 'Our responsibility, after all. Though I had no time at all today!' Nalini related how she had found them sitting together when she returned, with the boy helping Ranju with her homework. Rana did not like it, but curbed himself.

A little while later, he had changed into his kurta-pajamas and was pacing in the driveway, worried but outwardly controlled. Try as he might, he could not stop thinking about the worst possibilities – an accident, or something worse. Ah, the wages of parenthood...

It had turned dark before he heard the girls' voices, as they came closer. Then Ranju's voice, clearer now, shouting bye-bye to Nidhi, her close friend, who lived a few houses down the street, and then they were at the gate. His baby, with Mohan's son. 'Papa, I had a strawberry ice-cream!' She looked happy, and his voice thickened in his throat before he could wring out a 'it is so late...'. Ranjini laughed it off, and Ravi smiled lightly at him, and under his breath, 'these girls!' Then he asked 'uncle' about the train reservation. Rana replied about the confirmed booking in the Gomti Express for the next day, and saw the reaction on Ranju's face. Anger, and a choked, 'tomorrow only??' at her father, and then she strode off inside. The boy looked at Rana, helplessly, and then followed her with a, 'Ranju!' Rana looked up at the sky, dark thoughts entering his mind.

That night, he tried to explain his concern, and Nalini consoled him, unable to hide her smile at his paranoia. That Ranju is only 11, that Ravi is a cousin, more like an elder brother, and that it is understandable for her to look up to him. Also that if Rana continues like this, Ranju will sense it and – just to spite him – may become rebellious against his over-protective attitude. Rana understood, in a way, all that she said, but somewhere, at the back of his mind, he was uneasy.

• • •

1991 passed by and 1992 arrived. Ravi visited them once more during the middle of the year before going home for the summer vacation, but that time Mohan was also there. The boy seemed to have settled down in his college, and Mohan was his usual self. And as the days and months passed, Rana lost some of his unease. Meanwhile Ranjini was growing up, and requiring more attention, and at one point, Nalini even thought of leaving her university job. Pooran, their old full-time caretaker also decided to leave service around that same time; to return to his village near Raebareli to spend his old age there. So they had to search for maids and cooks to compensate for Pooran's absence. On top of all this, Rana landed two new contracts (now expanding beyond packaging of fertilizers, to insecticides and seeds as well). Finally, he recruited another assistant (he already had one full-time accountant), and tried to reduce his travelling and workload that way. They also managed to find a maidservant, and – with Gupta's help - a decent cook. So Nalini could continue her teaching, and they just-about managed both parenthood and careers. Just after her 13th birthday, looking at her interest, a Kathak teacher was also fixed for Ranjini. Rana would get overwhelmed (and teary) just watching her practice her dance steps. This was only when she allowed him to watch, of course; when she was in a good mood and happy with her 'Papa'.

In December of that year, when the Babri Mosque was brought down in Ayodhya, and there were sporadic riots around the country, Ravi's college closed down again, and he came over to Indira Nagar for some time before leaving for Delhi for an earlier-than-usual semester break. Rana got some time to talk to him then - and against his gut instinct - found him to be clear-headed and sensible; or at least that's the way Ravi portrayed himself. Rana took everyone out for *chaat* one evening in the car, and Ranju really seemed to be enjoying herself. Later, outside the Thakur Mishthan Bhandaar, as they stood to one side, while Ranju and Ravi went over to choose some mithai to take home, Nalini brought up the topic of a sibling for their daughter. Look how happy she looks, she said, and Rana had to remind her that Ranju may not feel as happy with a much-younger sibling. He smiled, she frowned back at him in mock-anger, and he realized he was still in love with her, the abiding attraction of hard-won love, familiarity and mutual acceptance.

That was the last time Ravi came to their house alone; at least as far as Rana knew. His work was keeping him busier, and as Ranjini grew up she withdrew into herself, which her mother accepted as natural. And that gave Rana a rationale for his reduced involvement in her life; something he could console himself with when she was away with friends or in her room alone. He was busy not just in his work, but also in managing the money that he was making, and then hiding parts of it from the tax authorities. Ravi graduated with his Computer Engineering degree in 1995, and after a brief visit with Mohan, apparently passed out of their lives for some time. In that visit, Mohan spoke more than his son (as usual) about future plans – about going abroad, or at least to an IIT, for his M. Tech., and that he does not need to immediately start working, etc. Ranjini was away at her dance practice when they came, and when their visit was mentioned at the dinner table, she was casual about it – yes, she knew.

• • •

Ramesh came to their house the first time on a Sunday morning in mid-July of 1997. Rana was reading the newspaper; about Lalu Yadav's arrest, and his wife being made the first woman chief minister of Bihar. Just another day in Indian politics. Ramesh had arrived with a letter from Pooran, from his village near Raebareli. Rana's first reaction was relief, because getting and maintaining a reliable maid and a cook was not proving to be easy at all. The boy looked small and under-nourished, but with bright eyes which made his face lively to look at. He was dark, thin and dressed in long shorts and an oversized t-shirt – used clothes, obviously. Rana called Nalini to meet the boy, and showed her the letter from Pooran. She gave him some water first, and only then read the letter. It explained that Ramesh's father - one of Pooran's cousins - had died recently, and that Ramesh had attended school enough to learn to read and write Hindi, but had never worked – except in the fields. Nalini was gentle with him, asking if Pooran is keeping well, and then whether Ramesh knows any work. In response Ramesh was shy, and only mumbled that he can do anything. 'Yes, but what can you do well?' Nalini was patient, and the boy opened up slowly. The boy added that he knows how to clean the house, and had some knowledge of plants and garden also. That made the final decision easier for Nalini – someone who could also take care of the few plants they had, and help with her now-growing interest. There was a brief discussion between the husband and wife about the risk of keeping a boy in the house, but considering everything, they decided to try him out.

Ranjini's initial reaction was negative, especially because of the presence of another person in the house, and in front of whom she may need to be more careful about how she dressed and behaved. But slowly Ramesh made his way into everyone's heart. Meanwhile, she had grown taller, with hair longer than Nalini's, a regal (but not supercilious) air, but still a baby in Rana's eyes (and heart). She had recently had her 16th birthday, and completed 10th grade as well, and with that her old uniform of blue skirt and a white shirt was also in the past. From the new session, she was going to start her Intermediate board classes at IT College.

Ranjini started teaching Ramesh – first some basic numbers, arithmetic operations, and then also English language. It was funny to see, because, besides being able to scroll his name in Hindi, he could not read it very well. They used to joke that he would probably be the only English-reading and speaking servant of his age in Lucknow. Ranjini had her own reason for this, but she did not know that Ramesh was also motivated to learn English for other reasons.

• • •

In 1999, they came face to face with two life-changing events. Ranjini had finished writing her board examinations, and was working hard on her engineering entrance tests. Nalini was busy with her teaching, and occasional travel. She had become a respected academician in the field of development economics, a Professor at the University, with guest lecturer-ships and administrative responsibilities. She was driving her own car now for more than a year, thus reducing her dependence on Rana for the commute. Her father had passed away in 1996 from a massive heart attack - after a decade long struggle with both diabetes and hypertension. After the death, there had been some discussion about Nalini's mother. "Chachi" had obviously not wanted to stay alone in the Paper Mill Colony flat, and after much deliberation – including about her health issues - moved with her other daughter to Dehradun, where Dr. Madhavi Joshi was now running a clinic together with her husband, and living with their children.

Nalini was now 50, and both she and Rana had – in the rush of life and work – overlooked risk-factors inherent in her health. She had put on some weight with age, but was otherwise active and happy, and their love seemed as strong as ever. So, when Nalini fell unconscious in the morning that day in April 1999, it was an opportunity to examine their life more closely. He had been kept busy with his work, and more recently with Ranjini's engineering entrance examinations. He rushed Nalini to the nearest Hospital in Indira Nagar, and they suggested her sugar be checked, and found it to be above 250 mg/dl! Some more tests and consultations, and so started the medication, diet control, and the emphasis on regular walking and exercise. Her lifestyle had to be changed, and Rana had to modify his own daily routine with her.

And then in the middle of all this, Ranjini's admission to REC Allahabad became confirmed. She had wanted only Computer Science, and based on her entrance test scores, could manage to get a seat there, besides some other institutes farther away, and so they agreed on the closest option. Rana went with her, once for the counselling session, and then to leave her at the hostel in August. She was eager, and a little anxious, and Rana tried hard to impart confidence to her – confidence in her own abilities and skills – and to tell her to focus on her studies and extra-stuff, and not to worry about her mother too much.

Once Ranjini settled down in her hostel and studies, Rana and Nalini actually found that they had the time to focus on their respective health, and having Ramesh at home helped. Rana started dropping Nalini again to college whenever she needed to go, and Nalini consciously reduced her workload and responsibilities at work. They made a new routine – of morning walks, healthier diet, and less time at work – for both of them. It worked well, at the beginning, but Nalini had to continue with medication because her sugar levels would not stay in control otherwise. In front of Rana's eyes, she started appearing more worried than ever. Perhaps it was because of her daughter moving away, Rana reasoned at first, but then found that her worry was more general, more inherent in her. A year later, her blood pressure also became a problem, and she had to start with medication for hypertension as well.

• • •

In May 2001, Ranjini came home for the summer vacation, and everything seemed better with her presence. Only for a while, though, because then came the wedding card in the post – "Ravi Mishra Weds Shreya Damodaran". In the evening, Rana called up Mohan to congratulate, and got all the news: about Ravi returning from the US after his Master's degree, and then the big revelation about this girl who had studied with him, and both of them would be living and working in Bangalore, and Mohan cracked some joke about having a Tamilian *bahu* and in-laws. Nalini took the phone then, and talked to Mohan and his wife, congratulating them, and excusing herself from attending the wedding, unfortunately because of her health.

A little later in the evening, at the dinner table, when they were talking about the wedding of Mohan's son, Rana noticed that Ranju was listless. Nalini tried to bring her out of this uncharacteristic shell by asking her if she would like to attend the wedding with her father. Ranju just made a face and remained distraught, and they let her be.

That night, when Nalini went to say good night to her daughter, she found Ranjini lying on her bed, sobbing. She called Rana, and as he came and stood at the door – unsure and worried - Nalini went in and sat next to her daughter, concerned despite her own health and the need for rest. She started by moving her fingers through Ranju's hair. Ranjini was initially unresponsive, but then her sobbing slowed down to a steadier breathing. Then, she turned her head sideways and looked up at mother, her eyes swollen from crying, but somewhat composed now. Nalini smiled down at her, and tried, 'do you want to talk about it? Or you will make us worry in suspense only?' Her smile broadened, and when the girl kept staring at her, her lips tightly shut, Nalini gave a pat on her back, 'tell me what happened!' Then she turned around and gestured at Rana to go away, mumbling, '... and close the door.' It was too much for him bear anyway – watching his daughter's face in such sorrow.

Rana woke up from his uneasy half-sleep when Nalini came back to bed. He rubbed his eyes and asked her, his voice hoarse and unreal at that late hour. Nalini shook her head, and told him to go back to sleep, 'will tell you in the morning.' She turned the light off, and as his eyes closed again, he heard her voice, 'our soon-to-be 20 year-old creation! She grew up and we did not even know it,' and he could make out a mix of affection, wonder and sadness in her words.

Early next morning, in the portico of their house, with a table fan whirring quietly, and sunlight falling on the pots of ferns and the flowering plants around them, Nalini looked tired but serene. She moved the newspaper away for the tea tray Rana brought. He had started making morning tea just recently, and though it invariably turned out a little too strong for her, she had started enjoying the ritual. She added a spoon of sugar for him (and none for herself), and handed the cup over. He took a sip of the tea, and picked up the newspaper, desultorily. 'Princess is still sleeping?' Nalini asked him, and he grunted a yes. Then they waited; Rana for her to tell him about the night, and Nalini for him to raise the topic again.

Ramesh came out to the courtyard from the side, and started watering the pots. Nalini watched him, - a healthier 15-year old now - and then got up to instruct – about how not to waste water, and pointing out some weeds that needed to be pulled. Ramesh had grown up since coming to their house about 4 years ago, and had put on some weight, so he did not look malnourished any more, at least. He had also learnt English, but never spoke in front of them, perhaps from embarrassment.

Finally, when Nalini returned to sit again, Rana put down the newspaper and looked at her enquiringly. 'So, what happened?' Nalini smiled, 'I will tell you, but you have to promise not to get angry unnecessarily!' 'Now, how can I do that without knowing...?' Rana felt anger building, but tried to control himself. Nalini waited till Ramesh had finished his job and gone inside. Then she leaned forward, 'our daughter is in love,' she whispered, and Rana looked back at her, dumbstruck. 'With whom?' he finally managed, and Nalini gave a resigned expression. 'With the boy whose wedding card we got yesterday - Mohan's son!'

This is the story Ranju had told her mother:

Initially, they just used to talk a lot (where, how – Rana interjected, but Nalini waved him down) and so found that they had a lot of interests in common. Ravi encouraged and appreciated her tastes – in music and books and movies – and they became really good friends by the time he completed his engineering degree in Lucknow. Then they started communicating through letters, and on some special occasions – phone calls. In 1996, when Ravi left for US, Ranjini was very sad, but he promised to write, and so their correspondence continued. In 1998, she confessed her love to Ravi in a letter (at the age of 17 - Rana remarked, in a tone of already having heard enough), and Ravi was all gentlemanly about it, though he said that he likes her too. Then Ravi started working in the US, and their communication continued over email once she went to college and got her own account. Ravi had told her about that girl (Shreya Damodaran), and 'he never really liked her at all; she was apparently very competitive and bitchy at work!' But then, since last year, his communication with Ranjini slowed down to a trickle, and the last email from him was about returning to India to work in Bangalore. Nothing about marriage, at all. And this is what really hurt Ranju; that he never once told her about this.

After finishing her story, Ranjini had sobbed for a long time. Her mother had consoled her. Her whole life is ahead of her, she is so smart and beautiful, she does not need a person like "that" in her life, etc., etc. Listening to his wife, Rana could not imagine handling such a situation himself.

Whether he would have had the patience to listen to his daughter's story without blowing up, without throwing curses at Mohan's son. Or even calling up Mohan to complain. But Rana also knew that all this was impractical. So he swallowed the bitter pill and comforted himself by consoling his daughter later that morning. Without asking her anything about it directly. He was not able to avoid it for very long though, because Ranjini told him the whole story. Later.

That summer though, none of them attended the wedding of Mohan's son.

CHAPTER IX

2003-2009

Ranjini completed her engineering degree in 2003, and had already told her parents that she wanted to work for some time before thinking of higher studies. After a brief period of searching around, and time spent with applications, phone calls and interviews, in September she finally joined NIIT in Gurgaon. It was a difficult period for her, as she had to adjust into a first job in a new city. Though Mohan Mishra still lived in Delhi, Ranjini was resolved to have nothing to do with that family anyway. Rana helped her find a rental home through his contacts – just across the border in Delhi. After four years of protected campus living, her new life brought independence with additional responsibility, and she tried hard to focus. The work itself was not very exciting – she had joined NIIT's Learning Administration team, and worked on helping set up Microsoft training modules. Her initial experience was that there was too much interpersonal interaction rather than a focus on software or training. And by the time her interaction at work stabilized, she was already looking for a change.

Ramesh also left the Rana household in Lucknow around *Vijayadashmi* in 2004. He had expressed a desire to learn driving and do outside work, and Nalini readily agreed. He was too young and full-of-promise to be working at home taking care of two middle-aged people. For some reason Ramesh did not want to become a car driver, and so Rana helped the boy join a construction equipment training through a contact. And so, when he left them after a decade together, a boy-shaped hole was created in the family. When Ranjini came home for Diwali holidays that year, she asked about Ramesh, but besides the obvious sense of loss of a household member, appeared relieved at his absence. Though Ramesh had been her confidant earlier – during the period of her secret correspondence with Ravi Mishra – she had lately started feeling uncomfortable in his presence, and as she put to her mother, whenever she was in Lucknow, Ramesh would be like a clingy pet, always hovering around and looking at her with pleading eyes. When Rana got to know of this, his first reaction was anger – why didn't Ranju share this earlier – but Nalini was more understanding, and dismissed any recrimination against the boy. Ranju agreed with her mother, and Rana left it at that.

In 2005, Ranjini landed a job at TCS, and moved back to Lucknow. Her parents were overjoyed, but she was busy, and growing distant – with her own set of friends and colleagues. Nalini's health continued to deteriorate, and after much debate and arguments, she finally took early retirement from the University. But she retained her innate interest in Cricket, and did not miss the T20 World Cup win of the India team against Pakistan in September 2007. After their dinner, as the match was reaching its conclusion in South Africa, she sat next to Rana in their drawing room, and cheered loudly when Pakistan lost their last wicket and MS Dhoni lifted the trophy. Ranju had also come over to stand next to them for the last over, and hugged her mother affectionately after the win. Rana felt overwhelmed, and could only smile.

• • •

That day in late July 2008 had started out with some hope, but it vanished quickly in the heat of desperation, and Rana felt himself growing suddenly old by the time the day ended. Nalini had been in the hospital since a week, but had shown some signs of improvement the previous night. Then, Ranju had told her father to go home and rest, and had stayed back at the hospital herself.

Rana got up in the morning surprisingly optimistic, and decided to have a cup of tea before calling Ranju on her phone. His phone rang before the cup was finished though. It was Ranju, and she was calm but serious – saying only that something is wrong, and he has to come immediately. So he took out the Honda Activa (Ranju was driving the car these days), and drove the short distance fast – his heart thudding, his mind telling him to be ready for anything, but not able to accept any of it. In the corridor outside the private room at the hospital, Ranju – somehow looking fresh and capable even after spending the night at the hospital – stood talking with a nurse. Rana stopped to talk to them, his mind already racing inside the room to look at his wife, his love, and they tried to explain – something about a ventricle leakage, and the situation too delicate to operate. Rana looked at his daughter, helplessness in his eyes, and she responded, readying herself to take charge of her father already.

By early afternoon, it was all over. Madhavi arrived with her son from Dehradun, leaving her husband and daughter behind, reaching just in time to see her sister breathe her last.

Then the cremation at Bhainsa Kund – in which Rana was a mere spectator. He seemed to have lost all capacity to think and act. Thankfully, his friend RK Gupta took over the practical aspects, and helped arrange the details. At the cremation ground, next to the Gomti River, there was a pause while they tried to decide who will give the flame to the pyre. Traditionally, it is the eldest son who does this, and the elders were discussing this, without much help from Rana, and were even considering Madhavi's son, Sunil as a contender. Ranjini overheard, and came forward assertively. There was no debate after that. She managed the rituals, her eyes watering from tears and the smoke. Immediately after this, Rana returned home with Gupta to a seemingly-empty house, while most of the others waited at the cremation ground.

As her mother's pyre burned to embers, Ranjini stood nearby for a while, her dupatta around her head, eyes partly-open towards the pyre, and half-closed with tears and memories. Sunil was nearby, protective but respectful – she was the older, more mature cousin after all. He was studying to be a doctor like his mother, and at 22, was capable, friendly, and suitably solemn right now.

Ranjini turned around and walked away slowly, towards the river, head still high, heart sinking, as she neared the now-dark waters of the river. Moving forward in a daze, she noticed a man there, standing very close to the water. At first, just a shape in white clothes, and then..., she realized with a shock that he may be about to jump into the river. Her own sorrow was forgotten as she hastened forward – 'wait...', and when he turned around, 'uncle, one minute.' The man stopped and stared curiously at her, as if searching for some sign of familiarity. He was old, wore a white kurta & pajama, and had unkempt hair, but the overall impression – somehow - was not of sloppiness or poverty. Ranjini was now close enough to make out that he had been crying, and said the first thing that came to her mind then, 'I lost my ma today.' Sunil had followed her, and was only a few steps behind. The old man came forward reluctantly, a light of revelation on his face, mumbling something under his breath. Sunil stepped next to Ranjini.

But they had nothing to fear here, because the old man collected himself soon enough, and expressed his condolences to Ranjini. After a few minutes of conversation, during which he also enquired what the two youngsters were doing, he said that he had to go, and handed Ranjini a visiting card – taking it out of the jute cloth bag hanging on his shoulder. Then he blessed them with a raised head, and walked away thoughtfully. Ranjini thought of stopping and asking what he had been doing at the cremation ground, but then decided against it. After a few minutes, they also left for home.

After a few days of dazed, coming-to-terms living, she related this whole experience to her father, once – she thought, though he was not sure - the pain had become slightly bearable for him to sit and talk. It was a Monday morning, and she was rejoining her office after being away for more than a week.

As she told her father about that fateful evening, Rana listened patiently, and finally asked her to be careful. He kissed her forehead then, and Ranjini was left wondering what she had to be careful about. Then she went back to work, tried to get busy with the usual routine in a bid to bear her personal loss, and it was a while before she remembered that evening again.

• • •

Rana tried to live on, always trying, and mostly failing, to cope with the chasm that had appeared in his life. Feeling unhinged, he would keep going back to the past. He had first seen Nalini in 1965, while in his first year BA at

Lucknow University. She was Mohan's younger cousin, a slight girl in blue-ribboned braids, eager about the world even then. And he had felt she was special, of course. He managed, somehow, to avoid becoming a *rakhi*-brother to her, as was the fate of some of Mohan's other friends. And it felt right. At least till the end of 1966, after which things fell apart in many ways. That evening at Kwality restaurant in early 1967 was the harbinger of everything! He failed the SSB, left Lucknow and everyone. Nalini and Arjun! And the taste of failure, one after the other. But then, Independence day 1979, when she agreed to his wooing, and they sat hand-in-hand, making plans for the marriage and after.

While Rana managed his grief, November arrived, and then the day Mumbai was attacked by terrorists. Rana and Ranjini sat and watched the news that evening, and the sense of frustration and helplessness would only worsen in the next two days, as the number of innocents killed kept rising, and live TV showed the counterattacks by the NSG commandoes. Ranjini took leave from work the next day, and gave company to Rana, who would get angry and aggrieved in turn. He called Nalini's sister Madhavi, who was traveling to Mumbai that week, and they felt relieved after hearing of her safety.

In the next few days, the stock market started dropping, and by the beginning of 2009, had fallen by 50%! The world seemed to be ending, and Rana was thankful for the tips he had received via his daughter, so that his losses were limited. More so because he had only limited exposure to the share market, having more faith in secure government savings and property assets. Meanwhile, Ranjini was getting busier at work, with frequent travels to Delhi, as the year proceeded. Manmohan Singh became the Prime Minister again after the general elections in May. In August, the surviving Mumbai attack terrorists were sentenced to death, thus bringing some closure in Rana's heart for the previous year's horrific murders. Soon after this, in late October 2009, his baby daughter (now 28 years of age!) surprised him by bringing a boy home for dinner.

• • •

That evening, Ranjini entered smiling at her father, and his heart gave a leap. She was dressed in her usual work attire of trousers and shirt, but today, more than ever, her face and expression brought the image of Nalini to his mind. And then she turned slightly, gestured at the boy behind her, and introduced him to her father – 'This is Neel. I already mentioned to you...', She paused awkwardly, and then the boy was in front of Rana. Almost the same height as Rana, lean, clean-shaven, boyish, but with eyes that appeared sad. He smiled very slightly, and held out his hand for a shake. Rana gripped his hand, and felt the strength of youth and confidence. Rana tried to speak, but could not manage anything other than a welcoming mumble. He was missing Nalini terribly, thinking that she would have known exactly what to do, how to talk, and which questions to ask.

Ranjini went inside to keep her bag away and to freshen up, and so it was left to Rana to be the host. Be the host to this stranger, who could be the one to take his daughter away from him! It was tough to remain unperturbed just thinking about it, but Rana tried hard.

Neel poured himself water, using the bottle and glasses kept on the center table, and asked Rana (in English) if he would like some. Rana agreed, and sipped at his glass thoughtfully, trying not to look directly at the boy. Who was restless as well, apparently, because he stood up again, and walked over to the wall where framed pictures were hanging. This wall display had been put together by Ranjini, with more photos added of her mother recently. There was a photo of Nalini from the 1970s, taken before her marriage to Arjun, in a *salwar*-suit, her hair tied in a bun, and a book in her hand. Black & white photo, which always reminded Rana of their days in the University (before Arjun Sharma had made his entry in their lives.) And then there were images captured of Nalini with Rana, Nalini with Ranjini, all three of them, and in larger groups of friends and relatives. Her whole life was represented there, and Neel stood and watched it all, one hand in his pocket, and the other ruffling his (own) hair. Rana felt obliged to go and stand next to the boy. 'She was...', he started, and Neel mumbled soothingly, that he knows, that "Ranji" has already told him. Rana stiffened at the nickname – the boy was already laying claim on Ranju by using a new identity for her, and Neel seemed to have noticed. He shrugged and smiled half-apologetically, 'sorry, everyone calls her "Ranji" at work.' Rana had to wave his hand dismissively, and then composed himself by pointing out the occasions or other people in the photos. Neel was laughing, as they looked together at a cry-baby photo of Ranjini in her blue & white frock, taken in 1986, during the early days of her schooling. 'This is priceless,' Neel said, and Rana could not help but smile. The boy seemed to be all right.

Then, Ranjini came back, biscuits and tea in a tray, and Neel took the tray from her hands and whispered something to her, and she gave a cry of mock-anger. Rana sat down on his favorite arm-chair, and the two of them sat on the sofa side by side. Ranjini brought over her father's tea cup and looking in his eyes, raised her eye-brows at him, as if trying to gauge his first impression. Rana smiled and nodded subtly. Ranju smiled back happily at him, and then turning around towards Neel, 'you wait till I see some of your baby photos, you just wait!'

As they sipped at their cups, and after a period of comfortable silence, Rana tried to initiate conversation.

'Where did you grow up, Neel?'

'Bombay, sir.'

'Oh, then you are far away from home, isn't it?'

'My mother shuttles between Bombay and Delhi, since I am working here.'

'And your father?' Rana could not help asking.

Neel was quite for a few seconds, and so was Ranjini, looking at him expectantly. She tried to start, but Neel mouthed 'its ok' and continued.

'Uncle, my father died before I was born.' And as Rana looked at him in surprise, he continued, 'He was on Air India flight 855, which crashed during take-off on the new year's day in 1978. I was born in July.' He looked down, and then at Nalini, who pursed her lips, and moved her hand to cover his, on the ruffled sofa fabric.

Rana noticed, but did not pay much heed. He was trying to search his memory, and came up blank.

'I don't... So sorry, beta. Was there a terrorist attack or something?' At the back of his mind, Rana tried to recall where he would have been at that time – probably between Calcutta and Lucknow, while trying for rapprochement with Nalini. Neel was still looking down, and Ranjini's hand was still over his. Rana looked briefly at Ranjini's face questioningly - why had she not given him some advance notice about this - but she was looking down at her hand. Finally, Neel shook his head, and started again.

'No. They explained it as "instrument failure and spatial disorientation". In less than 2 minutes after take-off, it hit the sea at an angle! All 213 people died. My dad – Mr

Haren Kotwal, was one of them. It was really weird.' His face was up by the time he completed his sentence, and he was trying to stay composed. Rana started getting up, and winced as his sciatica reminded him of its presence. Neel also stood up, a mix of youth in his posture and maturity on his face, and Rana held out his hand, and patted the boy's shoulder.

'Be brave, we are here for you. And now, you will have to excuse me for some time. Ranju, one minute.' Rana moved towards his room, and Ranjini followed him after nodding at Neel. Once inside, Rana sat down on his armchair, with an extra cushion under his hip, and addressed her.

'Ranju, really! You should have given me some advance information about this, this tragedy!' He made a mock-angry face, and smiled when Ranju frowned.

'The boy seems ok.' Rana continued, and Ranju's frown was wiped off.

'Really? Thank you so much!' She used sarcasm, once again. Ever since losing her mother, Ranjini had become more and more reliant on sarcasm as her main flavor of humor. She sat down next to him and Rana hugged her shoulder. He also decided to overlook the sarcasm.

'Welcome! And by the way, when and how did you meet this guy? You never told me anything.' Ranjini looked abashed at this, but tried to make up for the lapse.

'Papa! I only met him a few months ago. In March, when I had gone to Delhi for my new assignment. You remember I told you about that old man I had seen at Mom's funeral? He is only known as RG, he is an investor, with a big vision about Ed-Tech, and Neel moved to Delhi to work with him. Then RG was putting a team together for this new project "Vidya", and we met there. I was offered the role of Head of Development. That's why I left TCS, you know ...' Ranjini shrugged to demonstrate nonchalance, but her expression said otherwise. Rana thought he should agree.

'Ok beta, could you do one more thing for me before you go back to take care of the boy? Get me that heating pad from your room, I think you had stolen it from me last time.'

Ranjini laughed and went out to bring it for him.

After another hour, rejuvenated after the treatment and some stretching exercises, Rana rejoined the youngsters on the dining table, where food was being set up. It was good to see Neel helping out, or at least attempting to help, instead of just sitting back like royalty. The boy has had a good upbringing, Rana thought, and then remembered it as something Nalini would have said. No original thought left in him, it seemed. All good memories and thoughts stemmed from her.

Over dinner, they spoke of Neel's mother, and about his work. By the time dessert (*kheer*) arrived, a level of comfort was reached at the dinner table. After his school education in Bombay, Neel had gone to Nagpur for a computer science degree, and worked at Infosys in Pune for some time. At an Ed-Tech conference in Delhi, Neel met RG, the man Ranjini had also mentioned, and started working for their new venture, along with Ranjini, this year. Rana's respect for Neel's mother was bolstered, for bringing him up single-handedly, and doing such a good job of it so far.

Neel praised the *kheer*, and took some more.

CHAPTER X

2010-2016

Rana was arguing with his daughter that February evening in 2010. Already that year, 6 trains had derailed in UP, and there had been a bomb explosion in a Pune bakery just yesterday! But Ranjini had brought up the topic of moving to Delhi, and Rana had not taken it well.

'You are already travelling there every few days. Isn't that enough?'

'I go for a couple of days every alternate week, so a total of 4-5 days a month. But that's not the point! Vidya is growing, and I have to hire new people, and, ... and, we are also thinking...'

Rana interrupted her, 'but beta, is there nobody else? YOU have to do EVERY-thing?'

Ranjini simmered, 'but Papa, you know that every parent feels the same way.'

And Rana, thinking he had scored a point, 'yes, and what's wrong with thinking like every parent?'

Ranjini was not liking the way the conversation was going, 'nothing wrong, but you cannot also use it to persuade your 30-year old daughter to give up on better opportunities! And come on, Papa, you are in good health, and Delhi is so near.'

Rana was sullen now, 'you are not yet 30! And I still don't understand why you have to actually shift there.'

Ranjini forced herself to soften her approach, and came and sat down next to her father. There was something else she had not even mentioned yet, and so had to tread carefully.

'Papa, please understand: this is a big opportunity, and no one has been able to do it so far. There are development issues, user-interfaces have to be perfected, and matched with our pricing models. I have to be there.'

Rana stayed quiet, remembering Nalini, and thinking how easy it would have been with her around. But now, there was no one left. And Ranjini would become like a visitor, coming to Lucknow only on holidays. He looked at her, eyes ready to shed tears, and Ranjini noticed that. She touched his arm, and then hugged his shoulders. 'We will make it work. Somehow.' And then she brightened, 'how about you come and stay with us in Delhi?'

Rana took a moment to react, 'we will see, but what do you mean by "us"?'

Ranjini smiled, 'Oh yes, there is another thing. Don't be angry, but Neel and I have decided to get married.'

Rana felt overwhelmed, but he was not stupid, so managed to surprise her by his reaction, 'You should have told me that first! And before we finalize anything, that boy has to come and ask me first.' He showed a strict face to her first, and then suddenly, he was laughing, 'my little girl!' and hugged her tightly. Ranjini actually cried.

• • •

On the last day of that month, a Sunday, Neel made his way to Rana's house in Indira Nagar. He had caught the Shatabdi Express from Delhi that morning, and was feeling better than expected, having managed to get some sleep on the way. Chotu opened the door when the doorbell rang, and Ranjini, already on the phone with Neel till a minute ago, stayed inside.

Rana was sitting in the drawing room, trying to track the sunlight, as it moved towards the wall. He shook hands with

Neel, and they sat back down, making regular conversation. After Neel had drank some water and settled down, Rana asked him if he would like to eat something. But Neel had had a full lunch, and everybody kind of knew that, so it was just a formality. Rana then asked him, 'so… Neel? What is the program?'

'For tonight? I will see…' Neel pretended he did not understand the question.

'No, for the future.' Rana firmly brought the topic back on track.

'Uhhh, see, sir. I…' he fumbled, and then tried again, after a smile, 'Ranji told me to come and meet you.'

'I asked her to do that,' Rana tried to keep a straight face. Oh, how much Nalini would have enjoyed this, he was thinking and felt his eyes burning. Neel was speaking again.

'Ok. I, Neel Haren Kotwal, would like to formally ask your permission to marry your daughter Ranjini Singh, and solemnly promise to take care of her, in sickness and health, in good times and bad. My mother has already met Ranjini, and she also agrees to this proposal.'

He was smiling by the time he completed his statement, but Rana was lost in his thoughts. Unknown to Neel, Ranjini was standing in the doorway behind him, and heard the whole thing. She was smiling too, but waited for her father to say something. Finally, Rana shook his head, as if coming out of a dream, and raised his hands to bless them both. Later, he told Ranju that he was remembering his own meeting with Nalini's parents, and then their meeting with his mother.

'Come here,' he told Neel, and then they both stood up and hugged. Ranjini came forward and stood next to the two, somewhat shy now, till Rana pulled her and kissed her forehead.

So it was done. Rana joined them for a celebratory beer before dinner that day. They also discussed the actual wedding, and it was almost decided that there will be a court registration in Lucknow, followed by reception dinner, and a tentative guest-list was prepared.

• • •

Ranjini shifted to Delhi in March, and found a serviced apartment for the time being. Neel was staying in a PG since his move to Delhi, and together, they searched and finally fixed an apartment in Gurgaon, to start their married life there from June. It was a 2-bedroom apartment on the 1st floor of Galaxy, in Sector 4, near to the Delhi Border. Two things tilted the scale – relatively less dust compared to most Gurgaon societies in that budget, and a walking distance of less than 2 km to the Cyber Hub. They tried, but were able to only identify the basis furnishings till May, and decided to leave it for after their move-in. There was an empty plot on the south, and a wooded area on the West of the building, and their apartment's main windows faced West.

Rana visited Delhi for a couple of days, and the time he spent with Ranjini and Nalini reminded him of his own early days before he had married Nalini in Lucknow three decades ago. He also met Neel's mother – the fragile-looking Mrs. Ayesha Kotwal. She was born the same year as Nalini, and to Rana's eyes, appeared as a gentle, soft-spoken but decisive, and ultimately, somewhat eccentric, lady. But he was also gracious enough to ascribe her edginess to the pressures of being a single-mother, and perhaps inevitable, even natural. He just hoped she was not too possessive of her son.

• • •

Ranjini came home to Lucknow a week in advance of the wedding. She spent the time preparing for the big day with her father, and tried to catch up with some of her old friends (mostly already married) who were still in Lucknow. Neel arrived with his mother, along with a cousin, on 12th May. From the beginning, he had suggested booking a good hotel room, and though Rana would not hear of it initially, insisting that the couple should stay at the house in Indira Nagar only. Finally, better sense had prevailed, and a room had been booked for the couple, in the same hotel where Mrs. Kotwal, along with some of the out-station guests, were going to stay.

The court marriage took place on 14th May, at the Gomti Nagar Registration office. They had chosen to register their marriage under the Special Marriage Act, so there were no rituals to be performed. Only the couple, two witnesses each, and the court officials. Neel had dressed in a white shirt and khaki trousers, while Ranjini wore a pink cotton salwar-suit with Chikan-work on it. Inside the court room, sitting around, trying to stay cheerful in the newly-painted, but already shabby room, amid unending signatures on documents. Besides Neel and Ranjini, along with his mother and her father, they had a few friends there as witnesses. Finally, it was over, and everyone congratulated them, including the Marriage Registrar. It did not feel like much to her, but they had discussed and agreed on this procedure, so there was no complaining to be done to anyone.

After a lavish dinner at home, after everyone else had left, and Ranjini got up to go with Neel, it hit her suddenly. Rana hugged his daughter till her crying subsided, while Neel stood helpless with Mrs. Kotwal on one side. Then they were gone, and Rana cried alone, remembering Nalini even more.

Their wedding reception was planned the next evening, at the banquet hall at Novotel in Gomti Nagar. A guest list with about 100 people, with expenses shared equally by the two of them. It was a good gathering, with lots of welcome guests, including Nalini's sister with her son, Mohan (alone), and members of their Vidya-team from Delhi & Gurgaon. Rana asked why RG, the rich "godfather" (as Rana called him) and founder of Vidya could not make it to the wedding of his two favorite people, and Ranjini could only wonder. With the beautiful banquet arrangements, music, dressed-up guests, gifts and photography, it finally started feeling like the momentous occasion it was for her, and she managed to enjoy herself, with Neel by her side.

• • •

By the end of that month, after a 10-day holiday in Himachal Pradesh, they were back in Delhi, and got busy setting up their apartment in Gurgaon. Lots of shopping expeditions, for furnishing and décor and furniture and the never-ending effort to make the house a home. Ranjini tried to keep Rana updated through almost-daily phone calls, and whenever she missed, he would himself call and ask. She kept telling him to find some interesting occupation or a hobby to keep himself busy. Neel's mother was a more distant presence, though Ranjini felt she had established a good understanding with her, there were not many opportunities for heart-to-heart conversations. All in good time, she thought. Life was keeping them very busy, with Vidya and their personal life all happening at the same time.

Rana visited them in early 2011, this time as a father-in-law, and after a couple of days, Neel commented to her that he actually seemed to be very possessive of his daughter. Ranjini smiled at this, remembering Rana's worry that Neel's mother may be possessive of her son. It is a question of time, she consoled Neel. And herself.

When India won the World Cup on 02 April 2011, Rana called up Ranjini, and found that she had also been watching the match live! They discussed the game, and MSD's coolness, and congratulated each other on the phone. Nalini would have been proud of her training, and their resulting love for Cricket.

Days passed, as Vidya grew, and so did Neel and Ranjini's stake in it. As part of Vidya, they had initiated another start-up – VidyaLAYA – as the teaching arm. From the beginning, they had been wary of "coaching", at least the mass-market type, and focused more on specialized modules, for last-mile preparation of very select entrance and certification examinations. Mostly online, and with only minimal physical presence in cities you could count on one hand. Strong teaching fundamentals, coupled with innovative application technology. In mid-2012, when Ranjini told her father how much she was earning, Rana could not believe it, and even joked that it's not long when she can actually stop working!

In Dec 2012, Ranjini told her father a very strange story. About an adventure she actually had with her boss, RG, in Delhi. Rana was initially not interested, but Ranjini insisted on giving him the details. About her drive with RG in his car the previous evening. About a young couple RG told her to meet outside the PVR theatre in Saket, and then a ride to Dwarka in the car with the couple. And the explanation RG gave, about the girl being the daughter of someone he used to be in love with! Ranjini was very excited about the story, and though Rana made the right noises, he could feel a nagging sense of unease. Why did it remind him of something, someone, an event in the past maybe? You should meet RG, Ranjini said, and not for the first time. But to Rana, there appeared to be a conscious attempt by the famous "RG" to avoid meeting him. So what, he thought, he is not dying to meet the great man, anyway. He let it be.

In the next year, Rana came to know from Ranjini that they had sold the majority stake in VidyaLAYA to a large US-based Education company. And that Ranjini's share in this sale was itself in eight figures! He could not believe it, of course, till Ranjini's next visit to Lucknow, and she showed him her bank balance and investment portfolio! His treatment of her did not change, though he sometimes wondered how she managed to stay grounded amid all the riches. Neel was another matter, and Rana sometimes worried of their relationship.

But it continued without any apparent hassles, and Ranjini kept herself busy with Vidya. Narendra Modi became the PM in 2014. And Rana's health continued to be reasonably good as he approached his 70's. In January 2015, when US President Obama visited India to be the chief guest at the Republic Day parade, Ranjini called her father to tell him that RG was also invited to be there as part of the business delegation meeting the US officials. She sounded proud, and though Rana continued to be mystified, he exhibited only nonchalance.

• • •

And now, it is March 2016, and Ramesh, that useless fellow, has brought in a diary written by someone! Rana's head spins with the story told in it. About himself. And everyone else.

There is another timeline? And it was caused because of him, with a role played by someone called Arjun?

Part 3: Arjun's Agyatwaas

19 March 2016. Rana is distractedly fiddling with the newspaper again after finishing his breakfast of oats and fruits, when Chotu comes in to inform him about a visitor. Then he ushers in an old man - thinner, slightly taller, with less hair. Rana stares hard, trying to process the features. Of course! Given whatever he has read, and remembered so far, this has to be Arjun! How much crazier could reality become, after all?

Without getting up, Rana folds his palms in a welcoming gesture of welcome, his thin eyebrows rising, like questions thrown up in the air. Arjun comes over and covers Rana's palms with his own – 'I'm sorry..., about everything! But at least perhaps you can understand why I had to pretend to be in that train accident?' The smile is the same, though the physical appearance is very different. Rana had last seen him in 1969 – almost half-a-century ago!

Chotu is still standing to one side, waiting for instructions, and Rana asks him to make coffee. He looks enquiringly at Arjun to check if that is okay. Arjun sits back, and flexes his knee-joints painfully.

'No sugar for me, please. Rana sa'b, you have to believe me - every single word in that diary is true. You sent me here from another, ...uh, "timeline", and that changed things. For better or worse.'

CHAPTER XI

1966-1967

Arjun Saxena stepped through the gate to the past with a brown canvas bag on his shoulder. It was the afternoon of the 26th day of November 2015, and he was hoping this visit – his third – would be his last. In fact, he was counting on that! He was also understandably preoccupied with the recent death of Col Rana, his landlord and the man who had willed Arjun half of his assets. So much so, that he realized his mistake only after he had passed through. His diary was still with him! He had originally planned to leave it - safely packed in thick polythene - on "his" side of the time portal, by pushing it into a thin gap between the wall base and the ground, and thus to keep it safe for the few minutes he was going to be gone. The idea was to collect it when he returns back to "his" time.

But now? He had already passed through to the past, and felt sluggish. He thought, what is the need now to go back through the blasted gate again, leave the diary there, and then make the passage again? He might as well keep it. That way, he could read it any time he wanted – a way to remind him of where he is coming from.

Ok, let us see: it is 9th November here, in 1966. Shaking his head, he walked on through the (still-young) mango trees, on to the side street leading to the Faizabad road, and there it was – the tableau of the rickshaw, the lady (Nalini!) on it, and the man (Mohan) on the road. It was exactly the same as the last two times, and his eyes should have become used to the scene. Still, they stayed stuck on Nalini (dressed in pink & white) for most of it. He turned around from the departing rickshaw and asked Ram Aasray for a *kulhad* of tea, telling himself inside to feel brave - after all this is the third time around – and tried to chat casually with the chai-wala. Soon enough, Mohan crossed the road and joined them, and Arjun felt confident enough to ask him the best way to go to Aminabad. Mohan was aggressive, but his eyes were guarded, as he explained the options. Arjun thanked him, but could not think of anything else to say, and turned around. Mohan kept smoking. Till Arjun suddenly remembered the fate of the dog about to be run over by a train. He cursed inwardly at this annoying gift of precognition. Then Mohan also left (he is going to meet his "elder brother" – Arjun knew that), and he made conversation with Ram Aasray. He had some time to kill before the rendezvous with an about-to-die dog.

Finally, as he was getting ready to leave, Ram Aasray noticed Mohan's notepad next to the pot of water, and wondered aloud as to where that had come from. Arjun already had another copy (clone?) of that notepad with him (from his last visit), and so advised Ram to hold on to it, and consoled him that the owner will surely come back for it. Only when he picked up his shoulder bag, Arjun realized how heavy it was, and decided to leave it with Ram Aasray for the time being, while he went on the rescue mission. Ram Aasray was okay with it, and took it from Arjun's hands happily enough. 'Not more than half an hour,' Arjun said to him in Hindi, and received a quizzical look in return, but Ram Aasray was looking at the canvas bag. Perhaps the words Arjun had used in Hindi were incorrect? Or maybe the bag looked foreign?

He started walking towards Nishatganj, and crossed the family he had seen the first time. Arjun smiled at the toddler – fair, a head full of almost-brown hair, his tiny hand holding on to his father's trousers at the knee. The child smiled back, and Arjun felt unexplainable joy. Was the experience different this time? Arjun was not sure, and walked on, slowly, the green canopy of the trees on both sides very different from the present – which he had left a few minutes ago – but already feeling more familiar.

In a short while he was on his way back, with the job done. He had shooed away the dog from his sleeping place near the railway track, the train had passed by without any bloodshed. Once more! He could not let go of the weight of repetition. Then, as he neared the tree and could not see Ram Aasray for a moment, Arjun panicked - if my bag gets in the wrong hands..., cannot even imagine what kind of mess would be created here, in the past! But then, Ram Aasray stepped out from behind the tree, and gave him a welcoming nod. And, as he handed over the bag, Ram asked the question – has "*bhaiya ji*" come from "*Videsh*" somewhere? Arjun laughed it off, and waved goodbye.

He strolled towards IT College, looking at the colourful flowers over the arch of the entrance wistfully. It was just as amazingly beautiful as the last two times, but he had weightier matters on hand this time. Finally, he caught a rickshaw to go to Aminabad, to the Chedilal Dharmashala which Rana had suggested. The rickshaw moved on University Road, over the Gomti river, then narrow streets lined by old buildings, past Prakash Kulfi – looking like a hole-in-the-wall - and then turned near Aminabad chowk, where they had to ask for the dharmashala, and soon he was there. The apparently benign Lalaji manning the entrance looked at him inquisitively. Suspicious of the guest's appearance or his conversation, it was not easy to be sure. Perhaps he was just doing his job. Arjun signed his name as Arjun Sharma – remembering to write in Hindi - with a fictitious Allahabad address. The room was basic; a *charpai* covered with a thick *durree*, two stools, an open shelf in the wall, and nothing else. Bathroom was down the hall, shared with others. Which would possibly be the worst thing about the past, he feared, and hoped.

This was it then. He had come to the past and taken the first few steps towards settling down there (then?) Though it was for a short time only, Arjun found himself fearful of thinking about 'time' here. To get over that, he had to keep reminding himself of the windfall coming his way once he returned. After doing his job, that is. Arjun was determined about that at least.

Sleep took its time coming that first night – it was so quiet! And though too cold for a fan, he finally turned it on to get some circulation going. That, and for the whirring sound as well. Lalaji had helpfully given a large shawl-like sheet – and he used it to cover himself. The dreams were disturbing and confused, as was to be expected.

Arjun woke up nice and early (it was 10th November 1966!!) and except for the dirty business of using the toilet, he managed the morning well, he thought. A cup of hot tea, then "dry-cleaning" himself with cold water (there was no hot water available), Arjun changed into his other shirt, and went out to find breakfast. And found it around the street corner - *kachoris* with hot sweetened milk.

After breakfast, Arjun decided to take a walk to Hazratganj. He had not really felt like handling a Jeweller first thing in the morning, and thought it better to get familiar with the place (time!) a little more. The streets were emptier than he had ever seen them in his time – it was Dhanteras day, and people should have been out shopping for gold and metal – though the weather was sunny but cool. Maybe they will appear later. The gold chain was in his pocket, in a small baggy of its own, and he found it to be a perverse coincidence that he will be pawning (not buying!) a gold chain on Dhanteras! Hazratganj was different, barer, cleaner and relaxed. In place of the Janpath market was an old building, almost in ruins now, but still with a gate and a wall around it. There was a large church and school in front of a functional Mayfair cinema (morning show of "My Fair Lady"), but no grand Cathedral yet! Perhaps that's why the sky looked bigger. After a leisurely walk trying to make sense of the re-wound scenery he was witnessing, he took a rickshaw directly back to Khunkhunji Jewellers, for negotiating the pawning terms. The munim ji was gracious, especially after examining the chain closely, and happily agreed to hold the chain. He also calculated the current value of the chain at around Rs. 250, and offered Rs. 50 cash down, with provision for further cash as necessary, but only on a monthly basis.

By 4PM he was back at the dharmashala, with lunch in his stomach, cash in his pocket, and a bag with his purchases - some clothes, a pair of shoes, toiletries and stationery. He had completed his first 24 hours in the past. It was the same place, the same city, but very different from where he had been only a day ago. He had to now prepare for his visit to the University the next day.

That night (his second one in 1966), he could not go to sleep again till very late. First, following Rana's instructions, he had to put together the paperwork for tomorrow. Before leaving 2015, in the last few days, Arjun must have spent many hours and rupees in stationery and copying to arrange everything. The educational certificates were first made on the computer (using some originals that Rana had given), printed, copied on to yellowish card-stock, and then the signatures copied down on the "original" certificate. The new identity of "Arjun Sharma" had thus been created – with high school, intermediate, B.A. and M.A. certificates – as the man from Allahabad. Boy's High School in the Civil Lines and Allahabad University became his Alma Maters. Besides these certificates, he had also found and downloaded somebody's old Master's thesis "East India Company – Business and Conquest till 1857" from a public website, and made it his own.

Now, the fan was moving, the light (such as it was) was off, and everything was quiet outside, his file ready for the next day, and he had even decided what clothes to wear. But Arjun's mind was not at ease ("the mind is restless, Krishna"). Which was to be expected, right? And what was worrying him the most at that time? Not of being found out to be an imposter, nor of meeting (and making friends with) Nalini and Mohan, or just the fact that he was in the PAST!! What Arjun was really thinking about was how to face Rana again (younger by half-a-century) after having seen him die as an old man. He replayed their last conversation in his mind, and remembered Rana's face and his voice, the accumulated wisdom and curse of lonely old age. The resulting bitterness about life – how Rana had lived – and his desire to change it. Arjun ruminated till his mind was whirring from all these confusing thoughts. Finally, he got up and walked outside to clear his head before he could sleep, exhausted and overwhelmed.

Next morning was a Thursday, and *Choti* Diwali in 1966. Arjun dressed in clean pants and shirt, and with the paper file containing everything, got ready for the job "interview". He locked the door to the room, handed the key to Lalaji, and walked out on his mission. His other papers & notes were also in the file – though in a separate envelope, and not to be shown to anyone - and his iPod (with the earphones) was in his pocket. There was no way he could have left those in the room.

At the University, he went straight to the Faculty of Arts building, as planned. He had thought that walking into a department office would be difficult, but had not realized that his personality would appear like a "fountain of confidence" in the past. Perhaps his robust health and physical presence, his language (ease with English, and a more region-neutral Hindi) helped. Or perhaps the essential sham of his presence got mistaken for disarming honesty! He also discovered that people were less suspicious, the peons friendlier and less greedy, and for decently educated people (even those with fake degrees, haha) the competition may not be intolerable.

The peon - Ganga Prasad – conveyed the impression that he was single-handedly managing the whole history department. He was thin, middle-aged, serious but with an animated face, reminding Arjun of a sober version of Johnny Walker – the old actor and comedian. Arjun was respectful, and that helped because Prasad opened up during their chat. The HOD KK Dikshit and most others - including the Administrative officer (Ahmed bhai) - were on leave, and expected to be back only after Diwali. Only Professor Mukherjee and Dr Hasan had come in today, and Arjun saw no reason to meet them first. Those two were the senior faculty, and a little resentful of Dikshit's authority, it appeared. Ahmed was a lightweight in matters of faculty appointments, and the important thing was to impress Dikshit ji. All this was gathered from Ganga Prasad. Arjun left after wishing him a very happy Diwali (in Hindi, of course), and promising to be back on Monday.

From Thursday evening till Sunday night Arjun was by himself – in a city he had known so well, but which was mostly unrecognisable now (then!) The whole of Friday – Diwali day – he spent at the dharmashala, except venturing out twice for meals. Aminabad chowk was within walking distance, and so was Prakash Kulfi (though closed that day). Diwali night in 1966 appeared quieter than he had expected – though there were sporadic fireworks here and there, and occasional diyas lighting up the darkest parts of the streets.

For the rest of the weekend, Arjun roamed around the Imambara and Clock Tower, ate kababs and biryani in Aminabad, and walked along the Gomti river – from Hanuman Setu till the Nishatganj-end. On Sunday afternoon, he even dared to go to Chand Ganj and walk past Nisar Ahmed tailors, in the hope of seeing Nalini again. After all, she was one of the few people he "knew" in this city now. He could not see her though, and walked back to Ram Aasray for some tea and conversation.

When he was not roaming like a vagabond (or a tourist), he was sitting in his room and going through his notes – pages extracted from Wikipedia, a book on Indian History (by Percival Spear), and "his" Master's thesis. He had to be prepared for the interview on Monday.

• • •

Professor Dikshit turned out to be genial and overweight, with remarkable shell-frame glasses over sharp eyes, and the interview actually went very well. The only thing missing in his portfolio was a letter of introduction or reference. But the certificates, the thesis, his polished words, all combined to tilt the scale. He also had a lucky break - the most experienced teacher of modern Indian

History in the department had recently left for Punjab University. Dikshit asked Arjun to prepare for a demonstration lecture in the next few days, and then called Ahmed to introduce him. Ahmed was suave – trim moustache and beard, eyeglasses resting on a regal nose – and overly gentle. He offered Arjun tea at his desk, and they chatted of this and that. Arjun's personal story was well prepared, but Ahmed's mild manner actually lulled him enough to become careless in his conversation a bit, which caused him to fumble. Arjun apologised and gave the excuse of being "nervous", and Ahmed smiled understandingly, and said that he identified with the sentiment.

The demonstration class went smoothly enough, though there were some probing questions from three senior professors present. Arjun could not be sure, but imagined that his recent knowledge of the world (gathered from what was still in the future of people here), mixed with some kind of a mysterious sheen of a time-traveller, helped. It was smooth sailing after that. Arjun ran into Mohan Mishra in the department building, and introduced himself properly this time, casually reminding him of their meeting at Ram Asray's. Mohan was tongue-tied but friendly enough. Arjun Sharma got his appointment letter on 28 November, and then met Rana at the Indian Coffee House the next evening. It was so eerie to see Rana's younger version like that, and Arjun had to exert all his self-control to stop from blurting out something stupid! Though he almost did. The good part of the whole time-travel plan, Arjun thought then, was that he did not really have to make friends with Rana, only with Mohan, and by extension, with Nalini.

• • •

December passed by in working out the class schedule, handing over of the syllabus by the substitute teacher Atma Ram, and before the Christmas vacations started, Arjun had actually taught only three classes. The slow start to his workload was a relief because he still had to prepare a lot for those, and he realized that – even with respectful students in class – there is a limit to how much you could bullshit! During this time, he had also moved out of the Dharmshala and into the newly-constructed teachers' flats, next to the lush green of the university nursery. It was a big change, especially with the flush tank in the toilet (you pulled a chain hanging from it), cleaner surroundings, privacy, and the ease of walking for less than a kilometre to reach the history department.

Arjun was formally introduced to Nalini on 1st January 1967. It was a Sunday picnic planned by Mohan at the Prince of Wales Zoo – to which he had invited Rana and Nalini, besides some other friends. On that cold but sunny winter morning Arjun reached the zoo early, and was waiting next to the ticket counters when he saw Nalini, Mohan, and another girl (Shehnaz Rizvi) walking towards the entrance, and it struck him suddenly that there was something different about this. Not even with his so-called "girl-friend" Anjali from 2015 had he experienced this..., this fluttering of the heart! He shook his head – damn! He had an advantage over Nalini, having already seen her before, and knowing who she was – and that somehow felt cowardly to him. As she walked towards him, Shehnaz by her side, and Mohan a step ahead, but to one side, Arjun stood straight, and after a brief glance at the others, turned his eyes to her face. They were still a few feet away, and Nalini, having noticed the smile on Arjun's face, turned her gaze, self-conscious now. She wore a mustard-coloured kurta, a red shawl looped around her neck, a white cardigan, and the green cloth bag – her permanent companion, hanging over her left shoulder – bumping against her hip. She gathered the bag closer now, and looked directly back at Arjun. Then Mohan was close enough to stop, and turning around, introduced them. Arjun did not like the fact that he had to be the elder, a teacher, and so could only ask about their studies, as they chatted casually. But, at least he was not teaching either of them directly – he did not think he would have been able to manage if she was in his class! Rana also arrived soon after, and after the handshakes, Arjun offered to buy tickets for everyone, and they went inside. Soon Arjun became aware of Rana's obsessive surveillance of everything Nalini said or did, and then noticed Rana's suspicion of him - this new arrival on the scene. That perception made Arjun more hesitant in his interactions with Nalini, as he tried hard to focus his attention elsewhere, chatting more with Mohan, and with Shehnaz. He later realized that perhaps that piqued her interest further – his tentativeness adding to the air of mystery! After the stroll around the zoo and the picnic, as they rested near the exit, Mohan lighted a cigarette sitting next to him – after having asked if it was ok, "professor saab?" Arjun smiled his agreement, and noticed Rana and the girls a little distance away, eating peanuts, which Rana peeled for them. Pulling his eyes away with something like annoyance, he asked Mohan for a cigarette, adding, 'there is no law against Professors smoking with students, right!' Arjun had tried smoking in his own time, and never liked it. But it made some kind of sense now, and he did not miss Nalini watching him from far.

At the university, classes resumed the next day, a Monday. The campus became populated with students in colorful woolens, and Arjun became busy – with four classes of modern Indian history, and two of world history every week. Besides his work, his focus was on Mohan – the primary reason for being in the past – and he tried his best to spend time with his new-found friend. It was from Mohan that he got to know about Rana having passed the written exams, and he would be going for the SSB interviews in March. And it was Mohan who brought along Nalini a few times to meet him, nothing overt, just some mundane question – about career or studies. And so the friendship with Mohan – which he strove for – led to meetings with Nalini, and he could not help but notice her interest. The way, even among a group, how he would catch her looking at him, and how she gave undivided attention to whatever he was saying. He tried his best to keep his distance - after all, this is not what he had come here for – but it was not easy.

When Arjun had started out on his mission to change the past, the original plan (ironically suggested by the old Rana in 2015) was for Arjun to make friends with Mohan, pull him away from the young Rana's overbearing influence, and thus avoid the tragic (and hopefully avoidable) accident which was going to happen in March next year. Arjun added his own ingredient to this plan - a conscious build-up of Mohan's character and confidence. He thought that by getting help from, and then praising Mohan's taste (in clothes, movies, poetry and books) and so showing himself – a respectable senior, and a teacher to boot – as valuing Mohan's opinions, would bolster the boy's confidence so much that he could break away from a dependent and potentially self-destructive streak in his personality. Simplistic psychology, perhaps, assigning that accidental death to an over-dependent and potentially self-destructive "younger-brother-syndrome," but the plan seemed to be working. The only problem now seemed to be Mohan's attempt to force-fit Arjun in the place he had originally carved out for Rana. So, he still needed an elder-brother figure in his life, it appeared. And as Arjun got busier with Mohan, and as a side-effect inched just a little closer to Nalini, Rana got left behind. Arjun could see it happening – how Rana became (or was made) distanced, and his resulting frustration. Arjun did not like the way it was going, but it was another side-effect of the original plan, and he felt unable to stop it.

Then on to that day, in late February - at the department lawns where they were having tea and samosas – when Arjun sang a song. The last time he had sung on stage was in Roorkee in 2010, at some fresher's event – some ghazal by Jagjit Singh. And now, in 1967, sitting among colleagues (Professor Anand Kohli and Ahmed bhai), students (Nalini Shukla, Mohan Mishra, Shehnaz Rizvi, Arun Francis, Iqbal Khan and Ranjit Singh), and, of course, Ranveer Singh Rana! When Mohan suddenly brought up the subject of his singing, and the chorus of requests came at him, he searched desperately for something that would be appropriate for that time, and then his memory threw up the song that had come to his mind before – during his first trip to the past. He had later searched for it (in his time), and had found it was written by Gulzar and sung by Manna Dey – 'Jeevan se lambe hain bandhu, yeh jeevan ke raste...' Seemed fit for the occasion somehow, and so he tried it out slowly, at a lower pitch than the original, and then, once he got into the flow, continued for two stanzas, before stopping for breath. They were applauding, and his eyes found Nalini, who was smiling with obvious pleasure, and then turned towards Rana, whose mouth was pursed tightly while his hands clapped automatically.

In between, Arjun got busy teaching, and found that he liked it. He justified it to himself that this is the only way to live – that while you are in a situation, you try to make the best of it. And his plan was succeeding – Mohan was becoming a more confident personality in front of their very eyes. So what if Rana could not woo Nalini properly? That was not part of the deal Arjun had made. He only had to save Mohan from dying, that's it! The rationalization appeared flawless.

• • •

In March, Mohan confided in him that something had gone wrong between Rana and Nalini, and Rana has gone underground. They also knew that Rana was leaving for his SSB interviews on the 14th, and Mohan hoped that once he becomes an army officer, everything should be fine again. But then, a week after the interview date, Mohan came with the news came that Rana had somehow managed to fail the interviews, and was not coming back to Lucknow!

Arjun was stunned by the news, and after hours of mental struggle in solitude that evening, decided that the time had come to leave the past behind – and return to his own time. But he had obligations to the people he had met in this time, after all. Those people were making plans for a Holi celebration, and he should at least take part in those before departing. In any case, he had to ensure that Mohan did not end up dying on the 25th – that fateful day before Holi of 1967. At least his part of the deal would be complete then, he consoled himself. Best for him to leave after that, and let Rana work out his personal life.

Once the decision was made, his heart went out of teaching, and somehow he scraped through the classes. Thankfully, Wednesday was a holiday – for Bakrid, and then there was another holiday for Good Friday. On Tuesday, he went to Dr. Hasan's chamber, and to Ahmed bhai's office, and conveyed Eid-Mubarak to them in advance. He took leave from the university on Thursday, spending the time putting his thoughts in order, and settling his affairs for departure – finally planned for Sunday afternoon, on Holi day, 26 March 1967. He did not forget his duty though, of keeping tabs on Mohan – meeting him at their favorite kachori place in Nishatganj on Wednesday, and then at the Coffee house on Thursday.

On Friday morning, Nalini turned up at his doorstep. In his bare one-room teacher's flat, Arjun was still in his kurta-pajama that morning, having finished a breakfast of milk and bread (or double-roti, as everyone else called it). He was sitting down with his expense diary, to note down any pending payments, and to decide if it was worth taking care of them before his departure from this life/time. His file – with documents brought over from 2015 – was also scattered around, and so was the book on Indian history, by Percival Spear - the 2nd edition published in 1979! The knock on the door was low-key but insistent, and distracted with his thoughts, he got up and opened the door, coming face to face with Nalini and Shehnaz! He was disoriented for a few seconds, and passed a hand through his hair, trying to come to terms with the situation. With an effort, he smiled – not too widely – and Shehnaz started by apologizing, addressing him as "Sharma sir", and, 'hope we are not disturbing you?' Then Nalini added, 'sorry, but you were not at the department yesterday, and Ganga Prasad ji said you are not well...?' she trailed off, and Arjun realized they were still standing at the door. He invited them in, apologizing himself now, at the condition of the room, as he gathered the book and files and papers from the table hastily and took everything inside to dump on the bed, while he explained that it was just "some stomach problem – ate too many kachoris that day... much better now.' He came back, and asked them to sit – there were only two chairs – and pulled a stool for himself. He waved their hesitation off chivalrously, '...after all, special treatment for ladies,' smiled again, and they tried to make small talk. Shehnaz was in a bright orange suit, her round – and normally funny - face still apologetic. Nalini wore a white salwar-suit, the kurta embroidered with red and green prints, her hair swept back and held by a red band, and her green bag gathered in her lap. Her eyes were full of interest, her face full of life, as she looked directly at him – no apologies there - he felt a wave of depression pass over him. He is leaving on Sunday, he reminded himself. Something must have shown on Arjun's face, because her face reacted with worry, and he got up abruptly and asked them if they would like something. He could not offer tea since there was no milk left - and they were saying, no it is okay, anyway - but then he remembered the laddoos he had bought from Nishatganj that day, and so took out four in a small steel plate, filled two steel tumblers with water, and served them. 'Besan ke laddoo, hope you both like these?' The gracious host on the outside was kicking himself on the inside for getting so inextricably caught up in the past. He also took one laddoo – to prove that his stomach was better now, and as they talked – about Bakrid and Holi and Easter, and then about studies and being busy - he participated but remained distracted. Nalini noticed his distraction. He could see that too. They left soon afterwards.

The *Choti*-Holi celebration was scheduled on Saturday, March 25th, and was an all-male gathering. Between 5 and 6PM, some of them gathered at a shop in Chowk, and had *bhaang thandai.* Then the gang returned to the campus happily stoned, where others also joined, and they sat around singing songs and eating sweets in a university garden close to his flat. Anand Kohli, Ahmed Farooqui and Arjun represented the staff, and Mohan, Ranjit, Arun and Iqbal from the students' side. There were songs being sung now, and Arjun felt good enough to sing something which was still in the future – the very popular Holi song sung by Amitabh Bachchan in the movie "Silsila", to be released 15 years later – and the audience seemed to like its evocation of colours riding on coarse folk language. After some time, and long after the sun had set for the day, they went over to the main campus ground, where boys from the hostels had gathered some firewood, and there was *holika dahan* in a corner of the ground. Gulal colors, 'Holi *mubarak*' hugs, and back-slappings went on for some more time. Towards the end, Arjun and Mohan found themselves standing to one side, smoking and looking at the embers of the bonfire, and remembering the date, it struck Arjun that this was the day Mohan would have died in the other timeline! He looked over at the survivor fondly. As if on cue, Mohan started.

'Please don't mind me asking, Guruji, but what do you think about Nalini?' Arjun – still in a celebratory mode - raised a lazy, quizzical eyebrow, and Mohan continued, 'I mean... your feelings?'

Arjun was suddenly alert, shaken out of his fond lethargy, and said the first thing that came to his mind – 'but I thought our Ranveer was in love with her?'

Mohan laughed at this, 'Why elder-brother only? Everyone falls in love with her! The more important question is who she likes. Or loves.'

Arjun could only feign ignorance, and defensive now, 'that may be. But why are you asking me?' He had an inkling of what was coming. Mohan continued, flicking the cigarette into the dying bonfire.

'Because I am told by a reliable source that Nalini has fallen in love with our Professor Sharma.' Arjun started shaking his head, but Mohan was not done yet – 'and that reliable source has been instructed to find out how Guruji feels!' Mohan had a twisted smile on his face, and Arjun felt shocked. He is leaving this place – the blasted time itself – the very next day, and they have to throw this at him now? But Mohan was enjoying himself, '...in other words, is the fire equally lit on both sides?' Arjun's shock transformed into anger, and to control himself, he went over to the bonfire and picked up a stick, burning at one end. Kohli was shouting at him from a distance, 'shall we go, Sharma?' and Arjun shouted back, 'one minute!' Then he returned to Mohan, swinging the burning stick dangerously. His mind was made up, at least for now. The happy effect of the bhang had dissipated.

'Please go and tell your reliable source, Mohan, that, first of all, these things are done directly - not through messengers; and secondly, that the great "guruji" has another life, and that he could be leaving Lucknow very soon!' He was grinding his teeth as he talked, and then quietly patting Mohan's shoulder, he added a mumbled 'sorry', and walked over to Kohli. Mohan shouted plaintively in his wake, 'but going where, Guruji?'

That night was not easy. Arjun was tired from the exertions of the celebration, but the revelation about Nalini kept him awake and on the edge. There was no reason not to believe what Mohan had said, and he could not deny his elation at this knowledge: he was desired by Nalini! Of course, this is not why he had come here. This was not part of the deal he had made with Rana back in 'his' time! He had fulfilled his part of the deal in the sense that Mohan was still alive and kicking, but was he also responsible for getting Nalini to marry Rana? Maybe not! But how could he stop worrying about Rana's happiness? He had been promised those huge amounts of money in return of doing this. But now? Finally, sleep came after midnight. Holi *Mubarak*!

CHAPTER XII

1967-1977

On Holi morning, he sat down once more - with tea and his expense diary – perfunctorily checking that all essential debts were paid, and then keeping both away, thought again over the previous night's happenings. Now that he had blurted out to Mohan that he may be leaving Lucknow, Arjun had to think of a likely story. But before that, he picked up the diary again, and made a note of things he was going to carry back to 2015. His iPod (not working any more; some problem with charging), his polythene-wrapped diary of those few life-changing days, the keys to his rental room back in 2015, Percival Spear's history book, some loose pages of printouts, of course his "original" certificates, the HMT watch he had bought here, the two kurtas he had really grown to like (though whether he would wear those back in his time, he was not sure), and his wallet. That was it, he thought. Everything else – books, notes, clothes, etc. would stay here. Now, what story to tell people? The easiest would be that he has to go to Allahabad, where an old relative is dying and has called him urgently for some reason. Then he can disappear, and except for the department and some people (like Mohan, Nalini, a few other students, maybe even Rana), nobody would wait for him to return. And when he did not return, they will be surprised – might even make some enquiries – but they will not be devastated, he was sure of that. Nalini... yes, she may be hurt – if that blasted "reliable source" is to be believed, but that's a small price to pay for what he had set out to do.

While he was still working out how to implement his going-away plan, he heard his name being called out from outside, and so he put everything away and went to join the Holi gang. Newly-familiar faces, the joy of abandonment in colors and water, and then someone brought along *bhaang*-laced *barfis*, and they went around the campus, meeting and wishing people. This went on till lunch time, and he tried to lose himself in it, not having to worry about the evening, and not even considering going to Nalini's house (not too far from here) to wish her on Holi. Of course, he would never actually do that. Would send absolutely the wrong message. Mohan was not around today, which was a relief.

After returning, Arjun cleaned himself up of the colors as best as he could, and then slept soundly till about half past four in the afternoon. He discovered on waking up that he was very hungry, but there was no time for that now, so he picked up the checklist, packed everything in a cloth bag – and started out for IT College. On the way, he looked for, but did not find any open tea-stall. And then walking on to the mango grove, he decided to stop at Ram Asray's stall under the old Banyan tree. It looked abandoned, just like all the others, and Arjun sat down at the base of the tree and lit a cigarette – he had started keeping a pack and matches with him. It was quiet here in the late afternoon – most people would be sleeping off their revelry – and he tried to recollect the day he had appeared here, in this time, more than four months ago. Mentally preparing himself for the travel back to his time.

While thus involved, two thoughts struck him suddenly, unbidden, and he threw the cigarette away! The first was the memory of the gold chain he had pawned at Khunkhunji – he had forgotten about it completely – he should have taken it back! And the second thought made him actually stand up: RESET! Would everything reset here if he went back? Wasn't that the principle Rana had drilled into him? He remembered the dog who was about to get under the train, and cursed loudly. It was so confusing! He lighted another cigarette, and keeping the jhola down, started pacing. But wait! By being here and causing some changes – like helping Mohan survive an accidental death, and making (causing, whatever) Rana lose his military career – had he changed the future? That was the real principle, right? His blood ran cold just trying to imagine what he would see if he went back now. Would Rana still be alive? And what about Arjun Saxena? Would he even exist? His PAN card, election ID, bank cards, everything in his room back in 2015! What if there is no such room there anymore? He was so scared, he stopped pacing and came back to sit down, holding his head and trying to control himself. This is why he had felt so strange during his first and second visits. The universe was sending a message to him, and he had not listened to it! Great!!

After a few minutes, he got up and started walking back. Then he felt his empty hands, and hurried back to pick up his bag. He had no idea now about his next steps. He was caught here, in the past; that seemed to be the only conclusion. Because back in his future, there was no guarantee of a windfall from Rana's will, no job, no rented room near Nirala Nagar post office, perhaps no Arjun Saxena either. He kept walking, the bag hanging limply in his hand now, back across the IT College crossing, some spent-revelers hanging around here and there now, pedestrians and cyclists, all occupied in their own lives, and, then on to University road, a right turn into the campus, and only Arjun Sharma exists now – Professor

Sharma, "Guruji" – and he laughed, feeling half-mad, and after walking on auto-pilot for some time, found himself back at his flat. He unlocked the door – why had he carried his key with him, he wondered for a moment – and then inside the cursed room! He deposited his bag - useless now - on a chair, and stood, still unsure of what was happening, till he noticed the folded paper on the floor. It must have been slipped through the door while he was away. He unfolded and read - a note – asking him to meet urgently on Monday, a great opportunity for research to be discussed - signed KK Dikshit.

• • •

The "great" opportunity turned out to be a research grant from the British Council, with sizeable amount of research money, paper publications, and the possibility of a doctoral degree at the end of it. Dikshit ji had named Dr. Mukherjee as the primary and Sharma as the assistant researcher, perhaps also because of his perceived command over English, and British Council wanted the research report in English. Did anything matter now? It was all very unreal at first, but slowly Arjun found it to be a way out of his time-travel conundrums – the promise of work, extra pay, while adding to his qualification – if he managed to - and of forgetting about the past/future/whatever. Mohan appeared to be safe from any impending threat of death, and Arjun felt no real obligation to continue his vigilance anyway. Mohan's survival was not his concern anymore. Arjun threw himself into his work, and even stopped smoking as April came, passed by, and he remained confined to the department, the library, or his flat. Of course, he saw them on occasion at the campus – Mohan, Nalini and others – but did not seek nor encourage any direct contact.

But then, the university closed in May for summer vacations, and suddenly - since Dr. Mukherjee also left for a month-long vacation for Calcutta and Darjeeling - Arjun found himself free of any teaching or research obligations. Loneliness struck him harder then, as he started missing the people he had avoided for weeks now.

At first he coped with the solitude by drinking (whatever he could find), reading (history, philosophy, newspapers) and writing (class notes, poetry, random thoughts), some movies (hits like "Do Badan", "Mera Saya", and the vastly underrated "Anupama"), and started smoking again. After about ten days of this, he started telling himself that the situation was not as bad as he had earlier thought. Did he not have better career prospects now than he ever had in his time – in his other life till a few months ago? He now had a post-graduate degree (however counterfeit), and soon perhaps a doctorate. He had a respectable job as a teacher in a still-prestigious university, was earning well by the standards of the time - almost 350 per month - and had no liabilities at all. The only difference was that he had not been left crores of rupees in this time! He was even able to laugh at this absurdity now, which was a good sign. And then, the thought wafted down like soft feathers - perhaps he had better personal prospects too – in Nalini, of course. Aaaaaggghh, he cursed loudly, there was the matter of Rana! Now that he was stuck here, he thought he owed it to the past (or future, he was not sure) to try and bring them together. So, in that spirit, he started making plans to go to Bareilly, where, according to last reports, Rana had moved back into his parental home. Arjun first thought of talking to Mohan about this, but Mohan had left for Delhi to visit relatives. Anyway, Arjun went ahead and looked up the train timings, and decided on 2 June as the date. Preparing for the journey, at least gave him something concrete to do.

On 31 May, when he returned to his flat in the afternoon, he found a note tucked on his door. Only a few handwritten words in English – "Can we meet at Kwality today at 6? I have to talk." There was no name below, but there was no doubt about the sender, and in spite of his better judgement, his heart leapt.

Nalini was sitting at a corner table when he arrived at the café, and she was all alone. Sidestepping the usher at the entrance, he walked over, slipped into the opposite chair, and smiling, tried flippancy, 'see, I came.' She replied with an apology, a palm over her heart – 'I am sorry for calling you like this. Hope you did not mind...' and he responded, gallant - 'not at all. Only that...', and she interrupted, smiling a little herself – 'I didn't think you would be so busy nowadays, anyway,' and he, trying to be honest, 'no, not these days. It is only that I was surprised by your note.' Her eyebrows went up mockingly, 'really? You were surprised?' He only nodded, and then they ordered coffee and sweet rolls, as he tried to make himself comfortable – physically on the chair, and mentally in the situation. She was wearing the same white suit – flower embroidered – he had seen her in when she had come to his flat with Shehnaz that day in March. Except that her hair-band this time was white, and she was sporting large silver ear-rings. She stayed silent too, and finally, after a sip of water, he could not bear it any longer – 'so, you wanted to talk, Nalini?' She fiddled with a lock of hair at her neck, and looking up at a chandelier, in a lower voice, 'Mohan had spoken to you around Holi time...,' she stopped, turned her gaze on his face, 'I just wanted to find...?' There was a definite question-mark at the end there, and Arjun was caught now. After all, how much farther could a girl go, and still retain her self-respect. He understood that, but had to make an attempt, 'see, I always thought that Ranveer..., you know, he really liked you.' There was a pause then, as the coffee and rolls came, and even as he took a first sip, Arjun could see that she was eager to respond. But she also took a sip, and then, 'please tell me something – do you people ("*aap log*!!") think you are in a film, where you have to sacrifice for a friend? Is it that?' Arjun was taken aback by this question, and tried to show his surprise, but she was not done yet – 'Also, I know that Ranveer is not even your friend, so..., who are you sacrificing (*kurbani*) for?' Arjun had no answer to that, of course, and resting his forehead on an arm, he picked up the coffee again and looked at her. She had strong feelings about this, that was clear as the glow on her face, and he had to pick the words carefully. 'Okay, okay, he is not a close friend of mine, I admit. But, try to look at my point of view – I have come to Lucknow just recently... ('six months!' she interjected), ... yes, and you people ("*tum log*...") have known each other for much longer, ('how does that matter?' she mumbled in between), and who am I to...?' Arjun stopped finally, and gestured at her to taste the roll. They picked one each and bit it, careful not to spill too much. It tasted good, and after another bite, Arjun went back to the coffee and looked at her. She is a real tigress, he was thinking – and could not deny the feelings in his heart any more. Meanwhile, she had another question, '*achcha*, that Mohan, what was he saying - that you will be leaving Lucknow? What is the plan? When were you going to tell us?' Arjun was ready for that one, 'oh that? No, there was something urgent in Allahabad that I was thinking... but no. No plan now! I have a new research project, and I will be doing my PhD now with Dr. Mukherjee, so no question of going – at least till that is completed.' She showed her pleasure, 'congratulations! I did not know that at all. And how could I? You have no time for us students, anyway.' She was happy for now, and Arjun thought that the storm had passed. He had not answered her first question yet, of course.

And she came back to it. By then, the rolls were finished, only the crumbs left forlornly on the plates, and she was taking her last sip of the coffee, and after keeping back the cup gingerly, 'so, Professor saheb, what do you think?' He raised an eyebrow, still hedging, 'about...?' And Nalini, the bravest of all, and more confident now, 'about what Mohan said to you, that Shehnaz had asked him to find out?' Smiling lips, eager eyes, and Arjun saw no way out. 'See..., Nalini (he savored the name now), this is really very flattering, but let us get to know each other some more, isn't it?' He felt unsure if this was enough or not, and waited. She was collecting herself, but was obviously not in a mood to leave yet - 'fine, Professor Saheb, but how will we "get to know each other more"? For that, we will have to meet more, no?' He laughed and agreed, 'of course! Only one thing, please don't call me "Professor".' 'Then what should I say? ...Sharma ji?' She was happy, and laughing now, till he said, 'why not by name - "Arjun"?' That made her serious, somehow, and a little shy, and she looked away, 'okay..., but I cannot say that in front of others.'

They got up and he paid at the counter before going out, where he proposed they take a rickshaw, and that he will drop her home first. Then the rickshaw-ride; Nalini talking about enrolling in MA after graduating next year, and about her sister wanting to study medicine, and then the steep up-slope of the Hanuman-Setu, where he got down to make it easy for the rickshaw-wala to pull, and the cooler air over the bridge, then the wind on their faces as the rickshaw picked up speed down the other side of the bridge, and then passing the University, and Nalini laughing up at him, and their hands touching inadvertently, and Arjun feeling like a criminal, in spite of everything. Finally the left turn from the IT crossing, and then the rickshaw moving into the same lane he had navigated before – when he had seen her come out of the tailoring shop - and then she stopped the ride, and they got down, and she insisted on paying. 'Thank you! For meeting me, and for... for talking,' she said, and then added, under her breath, 'Arjun.' It felt so good to hear her say his name, and all he could say was, 'it was my pleasure, Nalini. See you later.' He turned around and walked back towards the campus, his heart beating harder. After a few feet, he turned, and she was standing and waving. He forgot about going to Bareilly after that. There is no stopping love from finding its course after all; somewhat like flowing water.

• • •

Arjun Sharma and Nalini Shukla could get married only after another two years, with his doctoral work keeping him busy, and Nalini wanting to complete her degree. In between, they would get away to meet in Hazratganj and other spots around the city. Their mutual favorite was the Botanical Gardens, with its ancient trees and naturally beautiful, not artificially-landscaped, gardens. Where they would walk and talk, Arjun feeling lighter than ever, though always cautious ("I am a time-traveler!"), and Nalini, happy and increasingly assertive about her place in the world. And Arjun started noticing some quirks in her behavior, but that only increased his affection for her.

A few days before the scheduled wedding date, Rana turned up in Lucknow, and through Mohan, arranged to meet Arjun. They met at the Coffee House, and Arjun tried to explain to Rana about his predicament, and also, not to give up hope. He was not sure why he added that. Anyway, it appeared that the two of them did manage to gain some kind of understanding, if not closure, before Rana left.

They got married on 14September, 1969, and went to Nainital for their honeymoon. Arjun was happier than he had ever thought possible, and he believed her to be the same. They moved into a larger flat the same year, Arjun got his doctorate degree (his thesis topic - "Siblings: The struggle for freedom and democracy in nations of the Indian Subcontinent"). after another year, and Nalini completed her MA (Economics) the following year after that. Life was good for the first few years. Blissful, even.

• • •

The worst part of marriage for Arjun was what he had to hide from Nalini. That he was not born a Brahmin, or that he had come from the future, those were his existential secrets, and so, more easily concealed. The physical things - his diary (still in its polythene bag) from 2015, the iPod and earphones (though basically useless now), Percival Spear's book (c1979!), and the printed pages from the future – were the more immediate ones. He decided to keep all this evidence from the future in a cloth-tied bundle, and kept it at the bottom of his trunk, in the hope that Nalini would not start fiddling through everything.

Even the existential secrets became difficult to keep as they got more intimate with each other. Marriages – the good ones, anyway - involve sharing of secret knowledge about each other. It is in the nature of the bond. He could explain away his atypical-Brahmanism by the made-up story of his parents' early death (which he had told everyone), and the influence of an agnostic uncle he grew up with (which he only made up for Nalini). She, in turn, tried to explain this to Chacha & Chachi (which was how Nalini addressed her parents) when they became too alarmed at his lack of respect for gods and rituals. It was Mr. Shukla who especially showed his disappointment that a "good Brahmin boy", who he had "allowed" his daughter to marry, turned out this way. Nalini's sister – Madhavi - was another matter. She became really close to her *Jija ji*, and found him a great source of encouragement in her efforts to become a doctor. Arjun also readily helped her financially in her studies at the medical college, and could have done more if Nalini had allowed.

The time-traveler part was a different matter, because it was at a more sub-conscious level. On many occasions, during a discussion, he would speak up about something that would later prove correct. Initially, it only validated his aura of being a very intelligent man. Singing a song from a movie which was yet to be released is a minor matter anyway, because by the time people came to know of it, you would be able to give a reasonable explanation – like in the case of the 1968 film "Ashirwaad", whose song he had sang in public in early-1967! It became more difficult once they got married, because Nalini was a constant presence - there to witness the truth of his claims. In early 1970, when he claimed that Amitabh Bachchan would become a great star, nobody believed him, but when the actor's films started becoming hits – one after another – Nalini also noticed. Or about Pakistan army's surrender in East Pakistan and the birth of Bangladesh as a country. Either he was just very intelligent, plus extraordinarily lucky, or he was prescient.

Nalini tended to go with the former opinion, because, who would seriously think about "prescience", anyway. Arjun also became more cautious in his predictions after 1971, but it was difficult for him to keep his mouth shut.

A few months after their marriage, Nalini had brought up the subject of a child. They had not actively attempted parenthood anyway, and Arjun's – mostly understated – argument was that their marriage was still young, Nalini was still studying, and once she started teaching – which she wanted – then they should revisit the question. He was, after all, a child of the 90s and 00's! Nalini completed 23 years of age in 1971, and received her MA degree later that year, before joining as a Lecturer at IT College. In early 1972, the couple went to Delhi for Mohan's wedding. The happy groom was now working in the Railways, and living in his service quarters with his parents and a much-younger brother. There were some other friends from Lucknow University who attended the wedding, but Rana was not there. Arjun and Nalini stayed at a guesthouse arranged through the university, and enjoyed the wedding festivities. During the reception Arjun got involved in a discussion with some of the guests about Pakistan. The popular opinion was that the Indian army should invade Pakistan, and take care of that problem once and for all. After all, Indira Gandhi was "a strong leader", and she had the will of the Indian people with her. Arjun contested the popular opinion and voiced confidently that an agreement will be signed soon between the two countries, and that would be good, because all of us required peace to develop further. Most of the participants expressed disbelief, or even laughed, but one of the more hot-headed guests challenged him as being anti-national for suggesting this. Nalini pulled Arjun away before it got too argumentative, and took him aside to introduce him to someone else. (Later that year, when the news about the Simla Agreement came, she remembered this conversation, and told herself that it is only because he is such an intelligent historian that Arjun had anticipated this.) In that same visit, Arjun and Mohan also got a chance to discuss about Rana, and Arjun came to know that Rana is in Calcutta, still unmarried, and apparently still bitter about life.

After their return from Mohan's wedding, Nalini brought up the topic of parenthood again, and Arjun agreed that if she was ready, they should try. But they did not succeed for some time, and slowly Arjun was coming to a decision that he cannot afford to have a child. He could not let go of the idea that he had done wrong – however inadvertently – with Rana. And gradually, as it happens, they both got busy with their lives and careers, teaching and research, especially when she moved to the University as a Lecturer – that parenthood kept getting postponed. Their intimacy suffered but love withstood the pressures of career and individuality. Meanwhile, the country also appeared to be going through its own crisis of adulthood. After months of unrest and news about the bad behavior of people - in power and on streets - that a national Emergency was suddenly announced by Mrs. Gandhi, and things went quiet. For common people, as long as they did not criticize the governments directly, life went on. The Sharmas were earning well and saving money for the future.

• • •

In the notes and printouts from 2015 that he had brought – and still preserved – were exhaustive notes about major events from each year since 1966 – accidents, crashes, political stuff, other milestones, etc. It was in 1973 that Arjun first thought of trying to stop a major disaster from happening. It was the Madras-Delhi Indian Airlines flight 440, coming in to land at Palam Airport around 10 in the evening of 31 May, with visibility almost nil because of dust and rain, crashing and catching fire. About 50 people dead. Rather, will die, unless Arjun took steps to prevent it from happening.

So, he wrote and posted letters to the Madras and Delhi offices of Indian Airlines. In the Madras letter, he raised doubts about the capability of the pilot of flight 440, and suggested he be removed from duty. In the letter to Delhi office, he spoke of his premonition of disaster on the night of 31 May, because of weather conditions. He tried different handwritings for the two letters, signed them using different names, and send them from different post offices. Arjun thought that was the only way he could make the airline authorities suspicious, and at least have them on some kind of alert.

It did not work. The accident was front page news on the first day of June. Just like he had recorded it on his list of disasters! So, there were limits to what you could do with the gift of premonition. It brought some kind of relief to Arjun to realize this. But he was not going to give up on all of them. Definitely not!

• • •

In the winter of 1976-77, Arjun actually started planning a future for Nalini in which he would not exist.

When he went for a conference in Delhi in early 1977, Arjun decided to carry his file of annual news summary along. There, he visited Mohan for dinner one evening, and got the update that Rana had still not married. That night, alone in the ICHR guesthouse, Arjun was going through his file from 2015 when he noticed an accident which caught his eye. Ahmedabad-Delhi express derailed on 24 November 1977; about a score dead – mostly from the upper class compartment, in which a Rajya Sabha MP was also travelling. Evidence of sabotage also found at the scene – probably the MP was the target. And thus was born the plan to stage-manage his death, and ultimately leave the path clear for Rana. Arjun was biologically 37 by now, three years older than his official age in the past. Nalini was 28, Rana 29. And the time-traveler had convinced himself by now that it would only get more stressful for Nalini without motherhood, and if he had to get out of her life, this was his chance.

His plan came together slowly. First, soon after his return from Delhi, he made a point of making sure Nalini was named as the nominee in all his bank accounts and in the few insurance policies he had bought till then. And then he put together all their financial details in one place, and showed and explained the details to her. He did this with the "innocent" explanation that – in any case - she should always be fully aware of their finances. By the middle of 1977 their savings were about 40,000; not a great amount by itself, but he was hopeful that with these savings, the compensation from the Government (for his "death" in the train accident), and some insurance money, Nalini should be well taken care of. Even if she never marries again, which he wanted, but also hoped would not happen.

In March, soon after the national Emergency was lifted, and elections were announced, they went to a political rally of the Janta Party – at the Begum Hazrat Mahal Park - with opposition leaders like George Fernandes and Atal Bihari Vajpayee in attendance. Nalini was a fan of ABV, and

Arjun commented that sure enough, Atal ji will become the Prime Minister one day. When Nalini said that he is only saying that to tease her, Arjun said yes, but he is also sure that Vajpayee will become the PM in 1998-99. Nalini laughed hard – a 20-year prediction! Anyway, the elections happened, and as a lot of people had expected, Indira Gandhi lost heavily, and the Janta Party came to power. Sharmas also celebrated by organizing a dinner party, with a number of faculty members, and some students, attending.

• • •

In September 1977, Nalini and Arjun celebrated their eighth wedding anniversary with dinner at Capoors' in Hazratganj. Vegetarian food, but with garlic and onions in it – rarely eaten at home, though Arjun kept trying to persuade her - which she had started relishing more recently. Towards the end of dinner, she slipped into a playful mood.

'So Sharma ji! Eight years, huh? How did you manage to withstand your wife so far?' She was smiling, glowing with satisfaction, and looking more beautiful than when he had first seen her. She wore a dark blue sari, her hair loose - falling around her shoulders and hiding the gold studs she had in her ears – and a blue blouse, her skin and hair shining in the lights. Arjun got caught up in those, and could only smile back.

'Nothing to say? But in your classroom, and all those conferences, I am told that it is difficult to keep you quiet!' She gave a playful push to his shoulder. He was wearing a khadi kurta and denims, his features now older and much less remarkable than they had appeared when he first came to the past. But he was happy with his life here, in his own way. If only he did not have to let it all go away... He pushed away the misgiving and spoke.

'Please do not speak like that. You have done all the "withstanding" in this marriage. I did not have to make any compromises, you know that. If I did not have you and your love in my life these last eight years, I don't know what....' She stopped him with a hand on his mouth. She had rinsed her hand in the finger bowl just then, and the fingers felt warm and moist, smelling of lemon.

'Don't say anything else, Arjun. I was only joking, ok? It is just that...,' she paused, and when he raised a concerned eyebrow, continued, 'that you seem to be a bit distant, perhaps quieter than usual these days. And I cannot help worrying. If something has happened at the department, or maybe in Allahabad..., you can tell me.' He managed to smile; he had to stop her from worrying. That time would soon come, but till then, he would have to make it as normal as possible.

'Nothing, really. Just regular work pressure, and then my travelling has also increased, and now there is this trip I have to go to Ahmedabad in November. That's all!' They sat quietly for some time, as he also washed his fingers in the warm water, and she smiled at him, as if understanding his concern. Smiling, he reminded her about a memory.

'Ok, leave all that; do you remember our evening meeting at Kwality about a decade ago? You were wearing blue that day also, right?' Their hands were touching now, and he did not want to leave her. Ever. Her fingers tightened around his as she spoke, cheerful now.

'It was not blue, Dr. Sharma, I wore white – it was the height of summer! Oh, I remember everything about that day, including our rickshaw-ride back home.' She was lost in her memory now, a hand under her chin, her eyes looking up, and hair falling over one side of her face.

'Oh yes, yes... White, with flowers embroidered on it. You had that kurta with you till very recently, right? And those silver earrings – dangling till your shoulder? I think I fell in love because of them. Really!' He laughed, and she made a face at his choice of words.

'You married me for my earring, *waah*!! Come on, let us go, and talk more at home. I will make some tea, and then...' They got up, Arjun paid the bill, and then they were outside. They walked past the new Janpath Market coming up at the site of some old ruins, and Arjun remembered the Janpath he used to visit year ago, in his other life. It was late, but there were some streetlights in the area, to help them find their motorcycle he had parked. A 250cc Yezdi, taken out mostly for special occasions like this. She held his hand as they reached closer, and he took the motorcycle off its stand, a few kicks to start it, and she was sitting behind him, her hair covered now by the end of her sari, her hand around his waist, and then they were off. The cooled-down night wind on his face, and the feel of her body, and when he used his left hand to remove her hair – which had flown in his face – she screamed, 'hold both handles!', and he laughed, and she squeezed his stomach, 'you are getting fat, Sharma ji!'.

Their love-making was tender and long that night. Arjun used to keep a mental record of her periods, and had estimated it was safe not to use protection. His time was coming to a closure (again!), and he could not afford to make a mistake now.

CHAPTER XIII

1977-1978

In early November 1977, almost exactly 11 years after he had pawned a gold chain at Khunkhunji Jewellers, he went there again. This was the only financial transaction he had kept secret from his wife so far. After some discussions, he sold off the chain, and received 1350 rupees, even after deducting the advance and some other charges. The gold rate had climbed more than five times during the intervening period, and was almost Rs. 480 per tola now! He needed this cash for starting out on his *Agyatwaas*, after all.

On the morning of 17th November, when leaving for Charbagh station, Arjun was almost in tears - he knew he was leaving Nalini for the last time. She must have noticed how he was trying to hide his dejection, and told him not to be so sad, and that he will be back soon with her. Finally, when he hugged her tightly before starting from home, Nalini had a sudden urge to stop him from going – a flash of foreboding in her heart – but she controlled herself somehow. They kissed, and then, once his rickshaw started, she murmured a prayer – to keep him safe and bring him back soon.

Arjun caught the Kamakhya-Gandhidham Express from Charbagh station, and after travelling for about 35 hours reached Ahmedabad on the evening of 18th. That same night, he booked a telegram - to be delivered to her the next morning: "Reached safely stop Will take AHD-HRD Mail arrive DEL-LKO 23 stop Love stop".

In Ahmedabad, Arjun found a hotel near the Gujarat University, as originally scheduled. Better to keep to the original plan. And though he tried to do some work, most of his time during those four days was spent in bed, choking his tears, worrying or sleeping. Is this all going to be worth it, he could not stop asking himself!

On the 22nd, after a dinner of *dhokla*, rice and sweet *daal*, Arjun went to the Railway station. He had his ticket with him – for the First class sleeper - from Ahmedabad to Delhi. At the last minute, he remembered and bought a platform ticket for 50p, which he kept in his shirt pocket. Then, on to the platform, from where the Ahmedabad mail was going to start. He waited, finishing two cups of tea and a cigarette with each, before the train chugged in. He had his leather folder in his hand, containing a half-empty pack of cigarettes, a newspaper, some history notes, his wallet - with the train ticket, his university identity card, cash and a photo of Nalini - and a small pack of Parle biscuits. He climbed into the First-class compartment, which was attached to the AC compartment (yes, there was an air-conditioned coach there, already!) on one side, and the postal van on the other. He went inside the still-empty coach, and sitting himself down on a berth near the window, pushed the folder on to the top berth – towards the darkest corner. He breathed in the air hungrily – imagining himself sleeping in this train and crashing in a few hours. Some passengers were now climbing aboard, and he got up casually, looked here and there – as if waiting for someone – and got down from the train. For a minute he hung around on the platform, his brain tingling with his knowledge of the fate of the people travelling in this compartment, and struggling with how to live with this knowledge. While planning for his departure from Nalini's life, he had convinced himself that it is best to make the minimal possible impact in this time, and not to consciously change anything. But, just like with that dog in November 1966, these deaths had become too immediate to overlook easily. He had to be strong with himself. There was no easy way to stop the train accident from happening, and anyway he had no idea when he would get another chance like this to disappear from his current life. With a lingering look, he walked away from the train, showing his platform ticket bravely at the exit.

• • •

The next two months passed by in a kind of limbo, while he tried to lose himself in the wide world in an attempt to forget that one name. The name that never left him, even after all that.

He started out from Ahmedabad after another few days, and reached Bombay around the beginning of December 1977. After Lucknow, Dadar felt like a jungle – people everywhere! He had been to Bombay in his other life – in 2008 on a college trip – but whatever memories he had of that time were already getting hazier.

Arjun found a room at a lodge, and stayed for a few weeks, making himself familiar with the people and places there. On the first day of 1978, he already knew that there was a going to be a plane crash of an Air India Dubai flight that evening. So, he called up the Santa Cruz airport number in the afternoon, and had planned to alert them about a bomb threat on flight 855, delaying the departure that way, and somehow avoiding the faulty take-off which lead to the crash. He used the phone at the lodge reception, while the receptionist was away from his post. After several attempts, when the call finally got connected, he asked for the airport security, and waited. Then, a gruff voice, speaking in Marathi.

'Hello! Who speaks?'

'Sir, this is a concerned citizen, calling about a security threat....' Arjun spoke in English, but was interrupted rudely.

'No English. Speak Marathi!'

'No Marathi, sir. Hindi?' Without waiting for an answer, he continued, trying to explain in Hindi.

'Air India flight 855, may be a bomb!' But the man on the other end was already talking to someone else, Arjun could hear the voice in Marathi, something about "Pawar saheb". He persisted.

'Sir, Bomb on flight 855!'

'What are you blabbering about? Wait...!' The man was dismissive, and distracted. The receiver was placed down, Arjun heard the thump, and then there were background conversations. He waited, getting annoyed by the minute, but still worrying about the more than 200 deaths about to happen in a few hours. After a few more agonizing seconds, someone picked up the receiver again, said hello, hello, and Arjun spoke up again, urgency in his voice, but the connection was scratchy, and the voice on the other end, frustratingly sluggish, now speaking in Hindi.

'Flight 855 in evening. Call later.' And the line was disconnected.

The receptionist returned, and looked at Arjun, who was sitting with his head in his hands near the phone. It did not appear that he had heard anything, though, and Arjun told him shortly to add the expense to his bill. He walked out of the lodge, looking for another phone to call the airport from. He walked towards Tilak Road, Dadar railway station on his left, and stopped when he noticed a red telephone box, mounted on the wall between a travel agency on one side and some office on the other. There was a thin, bearded man sitting on a stool next to it, reading a Marathi newspaper, and raised his head at Arjun. Gesturing at the phone, Arjun raised his eyebrows, and the man gave a nod, mumbling something in Marathi, which sounded to Arjun like "Chai"! He walked over and lifted the cradle. There was no tone, and Arjun pressed the lever, twice, thrice, till the beard spoke out again, this time in Hindi.

'Oh, line must be closed now, come back later.'

Later in the evening, Arjun ventured out again, the memory of those dead (about to die!) pulling at his nerves. It was getting close to 7PM, and he had to make that call now. This time, there were 3 police constables standing near to the phone box, smoking bidis, and talking to the bearded man. For all I know, the phone may be working perfectly, Arjun thought and cursed. There was no way else now, but to try and find another phone.

His performance for the rest of that frustrating evening: found 5 more public phones in the Dadar area, connected with the airport 3 times, but could speak to someone at the other end just once. And that person just laughed, like a demon, and left the receiver off, while going away for something important. At 8PM, Arjun gave up. He could not be realistically expected to achieve everything he sets out for, even with precognition and all! He rationalized, as he read about the crash the next morning. As scheduled.

• • •

Arjun went to Khandala, where it was really cold at that time, and liked it so much, it triggered a search for the mountains, likely somewhere in the North. Khandala was becoming popular, film stars had started buying land and building huge bungalows as summer homes. Then he travelled to Pune, wandering around the city, including the Acharya Rajneesh ashram. Arjun remembered what he had known about Rajneesh, including his legal problems in the US, and then death after his return to India. While he roamed around in this timeline, the ashram property appeared beautifully maintained, though he also picked up rumours of government investigations starting on the Acharya and his gang.

While in Poona, Arjun visited Mahabaleshwar, Alibaug and the western coast, taking his time, still in a daze, but slowly coming to terms with his wanderer side. In mid-January 1978, he took a train from Poona to Delhi. Delhi was cold and bleak – the Janata Party government doing its best to be a killjoy. After days spent searching around newspaper offices and schools, he started thinking about the mountains again. There was only one saleable (and legal) talent he had now – teaching - and where better to use it than somewhere in Kumaon? He did his research first, finding maps and locations and potential places to live. And from his several visits to the offices of the Education ministry, he also managed to find some names that he could throw for effect.

In early February, he arrived in Kathgodam, and took a bus to Bhimtal. After a couple of days of acclimatization, he walked over to the Devi *ka* Mandir outside town, and met Joshi ji, the elderly priest at the temple. The Pujari was the elder brother of the Principal at Government School at NalDamyanti Tal. Arjun related a sad story to the old Pujari – culminating in a desire to leave big cities (like Lucknow) and helping the society directly. He also spoke about (and showed the certificates made in 2015!) his higher education from Allahabad, a promising career beginning in

Lucknow, but abruptly cut short by personal loss, because of which he wanted to get away from it all. The elderly Joshi ji was sympathetic, and told him to meet his brother at the school. After a few days – during which the Headmaster assessed and observed him closely - he got a job as a teacher, with a salary of 175 rupees, and free food during the day. Arjun found a place to stay nearby, and settled down. At least till August, when he had some work to complete in Delhi.

• • •

Arjun was in Delhi again on 23 August 1978. It was raining, and that did not help his spirits at all. By the fag end of the period since leaving Lucknow, and even as he had started teaching village children basic arithmetic and social studies, there was one intention which had become clearer in his mind - like a ray of sunlight highlighting dust motes in an otherwise darkened room. This was the first of the really evil crimes that he had researched the most, back in 2015. His failure with the flight disaster was dejecting, but this was a crime; more immediate, personal, and hopefully, more controllable. So he had compiled most information about this one crime. Except for one more, which was much farther still in the new future. And Arjun had resolved to make this difference - whatever happens to the two murderers afterwards – and there was no way of being sure that they would not commit another crime of the same magnitude - at least he could save the two teenagers from their ordeal and death! He felt sure the parents would not mind it at all that the national bravery award would be named after someone else.

He waited at the Delhi railway station till the rain stopped. While waiting, he asked around, and found the name of a small hotel nearby on the Paharganj side, and found a rickshaw to take him there. His first aim was to make himself comfortable, and get some rest before the real work started. That day and the next, he stayed in the room and tried to make himself familiar with the map of Delhi. The next day, he shaved, got a haircut, and generally made himself presentable. That same evening he went to Dhaula Kuan for a rehearsal round. Walking around, and making small marks on his map, he observed the area around the bus stand, which was a few feet away from the entrance to Delhi cantonment. Then he took a taxi to go to Prasar Bhavan, the office of the All India Radio, not too far from the Parliament building. He asked the driver to first go to the Gole Daak Khana – the GPO, and once they reached there, decided to get down and walk to the AIR office, a distance of about one kilometre. If only the siblings had walked to Prasar Bhavan, he thought, and then corrected himself – it was yet to happen! He looked at his watch; in another 48 hours to be exact.

The next day, a Friday, he spent in his room, only going out once for lunch. He knew where Mohan lived, but there was no question of contacting him or anyone else. For now, nothing else existed – not his past, nor his future. It was only today. In the evening, he caught a taxi again – from near the station, to go to Dhaula Kuan. He timed the ride, and asked the driver to tell him the distance also. 22 minutes, 10 km. After noting these down, he asked the driver to turn around and take him to Gole Daak Khana. 14 minutes, 7 km. He got down there and walked around, stopping at a tea stall to finalize his plan.

So, this was it: he had to reach the Dhaula Kuan bus stand before 6:15PM on Saturday, keep the taxi running, then pick up the brother and sister from the stand (he still had to make up a convincing story about that), and drop them to Prasar Bhavan. In case he missed them at Dhaula Kuan, the second chance he had was to pick them up from Gole Daak Khana roundabout, and if even that failed (and he worried about this the most), then he would have to go to Buddha Jayanti park and try to stop them from being killed. After that, he was free – to go on with his newly chosen life. He had a ticket booked on the Kathgodam Express train for Sunday night. Back to his schoolteacher life.

He got drunk that night. There were very few options available to distract himself with, anyway. Next day – Saturday, 25 August 1977 - he prepared himself for the evening, taking out his best set of pants and shirt, getting them pressed, resting and exercising in his small hotel room otherwise. He also worked out the speech - about what he would say to the children when he picked them up from the bus stand. He took a nap again after lunch, and woke up with a start around 3:30 – after some terrible nightmare, but he could not remember the details. He shaved and took bath, and then walked outside for tea and smoke. By 4:30, he was back in the room, and for want of anything else, he went through the Wikipedia notes again – police report of the crime and eyewitness accounts. As he read, he realized that he was shivering, and ascribed it to a mix of fright and elation. Another cigarette, and then while washing his face again, he looked in the mirror. He looked presentable and reliable enough, he thought, though there were signs of tension and worry around his eyes and forehead. Hopefully only to his own eyes. At 5:30PM he locked the room and came down.

For a few minutes, as he walked slowly towards the station entrance and could not see any taxi around, his anxiety increased. The clock was ticking..., and then, finally - a taxi going the opposite way; he waved desperately, and it stopped. Arjun asked him, and climbed in. 5:46PM, he noticed, and then the taxi turned around and they were moving. Arjun sat with an elbow at the window, mouthing silently what he would say to the brother-sister duo. After a few minutes, the taxi slowed down, and then came to a stop. He could see the Birla Mandir spires on the right side of the road, and there was a large crowd in front of them. The driver asked a man standing with his cycle to one side, and they came to know that there was some VIP visitor there. After a few moments of waiting, they started inching forward – people were shouting and trying to clear the way – but it was slow. Arjun was scared of looking at his watch, but could not resist – almost 6PM! Another few, heart-stopping minutes, and then they were moving freely, crossing the Wellingdon hospital roundabout, and then the President's House and the Parliament on their left, and moving faster now, and Arjun felt hopeful. They turned right at Sardar Patel Marg, and then in a few more minutes, as Arjun sat forward now, on the edge, he could see the Dhaula Kuan signal in front. They had to stop for the red light, and Arjun looked at his watch – 6:11 already! It started drizzling slightly as the light turned green and they lurched forward, and Arjun leaned over to look towards the right side of the road – nobody there yet. They crossed the bus stand, and then Arjun asked the driver to take a U-turn, and at 6:14 they stopped. Arjun had earlier identified a clear area a few feet before the bus stand, and told the driver to keep the meter running, and that he had to pick someone up. They waited, Arjun holding his breath.

And then the two children – the older girl who looked as if she was always busy managing situations, and the taller but younger boy with a guitar slung on his shoulder - walked out of the cantonment entrance, and walked to the bus stand almost in slow motion. Arjun opened the taxi door and telling the driver to wait, got out. The taxi driver was hesitant, 'should I bring the vehicle forward?' Arjun told him to stay there, and walked eagerly forward, and then consciously slowing down to an easier walk. He could feel the drizzle falling lightly on him, and as he neared the children, he noticed their features, the innocence of age and the good living of army cantonment life on their faces and clothes and posture. He forced himself to smile, and then spoke in English, 'hello kids! You are Captain Chopra's children, right?' The boy seemed confused by the question, and moved back a few inches. The girl smiled brightly though, replying with a, 'Yes uncle ji! How do you...?' Arjun interrupted her, gently, not wanting to go there, and 'I am his friend – Arjun Sharma.' Then he smiled again and waved at the boy, who, finally smiled back. 'He asked me to drop you two to the AIR building. You have a program today, it seems?' The children became friendlier now, agreeing with him, though the girl tried to be modest about the program itself – '...small thing only! We were waiting for the bus, actually.' Arjun turned around and gestured at the taxi driver to come forward now, and then told them, 'some problem with the bus service today, I heard, so...'

A blue Premier car drove by, as Arjun got into the front seat of the taxi, offering them to sit comfortably in the back, and then they were off. That must be the car that would have given them a lift till Gole Daak Khana, from where they would be picked up by Ranga and Billa! If he was not here today. Arjun felt strange, disembodied, as he heard himself tell the taxi driver to go to All India Radio. It was still raining, and the smell of wet earth wafted up. The children were talking in the back, and he looked out the window, feeling like smoking now. In fact, given the time and place, he could have smoked freely and no one would have said anything to him. He shook his head, and turned around, as he heard the boy addressing him as "uncle". 'How do you know daddy?' Arjun smiled back at him, and the girl looking indulgently at her brother, 'from college. Your daddy and I studied together.' The boy brightened, 'oh, you also went to Hansraj?' Arjun nodded and started turning around, when the girl spoke up, 'you live in Delhi, uncle?' And Arjun swiveled back again, 'no, fortunately. I live in the mountains.' He smiled before turning around and sitting straight again. After a few minutes of silence, Arjun could hear the boy humming under his breath – likely rehearsing his song – and his head started aching. The headache was surprising because he actually felt so relieved he could burst into a song himself, he thought. And then they were turning onto Ashoka Road, and the broadcasting house building could be seen now. 'Thank you so much, uncle!' the girl was speaking from the back, and Arjun just mumbled to himself, 'you are most welcome.' The taxi stopped in front of the gate, and the children started getting out. Arjun debated with himself for a second, and then got out himself. 'Good luck with your program,' he heard himself say, and stood, uncertain of what to do next. The drizzle had almost stopped. The boy said "thank you" and started walking towards the gate, but the girl lingered, 'you should come home sometime, uncle, before you go back to your mountains.' She was pleasantly pretty, and Arjun's eyes watered just thinking about the terrible experiences she had avoided. Today, at least. Because who knows? Even he did not. He turned around abruptly, 'sure, I will talk to Chopra soon.' She turned around too, and he sat back in the taxi, and waited till they were both inside the gate. He sighed then, and sat for a few moments like that, till the taxi driver asked, 'where now?' 'Connaught Place', he said without thinking much, and they started.

Even before they had moved a few feet, Arjun reconsidered his decision, and told the driver to go to Gole Daak Khana, near the Yogashram gate. So the taxi turned left at Patel chowk, and in a few short minutes, they were there. Even as he got down and paid, he was looking around, at the cars moving around – searching for the yellow-brown Fiat car with two people in the front. Where he had gotten down, Ashoka road met the GPO roundabout, the imposing building in the middle of the grassy area. He was standing at the entrance to the Yogashram, the Bangla Sahib Gurudwara at his back, and he could see four other roads radiating out from the roundabout. And then he noticed a dusty Fiat coming into the roundabout from Baba Kharak Singh marg, crossing the Gurudwara, and coming closer. He froze, trying to catch a glimpse of the occupants – there were two in the front seat – and he felt sure it was them! Even as he realized that, he noticed them slowing, and then moving past him, on around the roundabout, making another circuit, and still looking for potential victims. He knew that Billa and Ranga had stolen the car for this very purpose – to kidnap somebody rich (and vulnerable) enough to get some ransom from - and it looks like they were still searching. This was the reason he had come here, after all. He had saved the children from certain death, yes, but what if these bastards picked up someone else? If he could just manage to thwart one attempt, they might actually become wary of it and give up

– at least for today.

And then he noticed a woman and a child coming from the next road to his left, walking towards the roundabout, umbrella in the mother's hand, ready to secure her son if needed. Yellow sari, purse on her shoulder, and the well-dressed little boy by her side. Obviously middle-class, and defenseless enough to be at risk from the desperate duo. He turned around to check, and noticed the Fiat coming around again, still on the prowl. They would have seen the mother and child by now, he worried, and started crossing the road quickly. It was starting to drizzle again, and he could see the woman open up the umbrella, and pull her son closer. They were standing at the edge of the road, waiting for conveyance of some kind. Arjun could see them clearly now, and then the car passed him by, and was slowing down – near the mother and her son. He could see one head leaning out and talking to the woman, and he was still a few feet away. He did the first thing that came to his mind, and shouted, 'bhabhi ji!' She heard him, turned around, and Arjun folded his hands at her, smiling and moving closer. She looked prosperous, plump and fair, but he felt confident that she would not be suspicious of him, at least. So he decided to dispense with the killers first. Moving closer to the car, he asked loudly, '*haan bhai*, where are you going?' The face in the open window looked plain and cruel – perhaps only because Arjun knew about him - and answered, 'nowhere sa'b ji! Just trying to help.' And Arjun decided to dismiss him with an offhand, 'hope vehicle has all the papers...' and turned towards the woman and her son. 'Bhabhi ji', he started again, 'sorry, I saw you from far, and thought perhaps some help...' The car had started moving by now, and he turned around just enough to see them off. Perhaps this will cool their blood-lust for the time being.

The woman was looking at him enquiringly, the umbrella still above her head, her son's hand held tightly in her other hand. 'You... sorry..., I did not recognize....' Arjun, pretending surprise – 'oh, you must have forgotten! I work with bhaisab. We had met last year... "bete ji" has grown so much since then!' and patted the boy's head affectionately. The woman still looked confused, but smiled apologetically, and so he continued, 'but what are you doing here, alone? Going somewhere?' And she first tried to explain, slowly starting to unload her frustrations - how she had come to see someone at the hospital, and now had to go to Shankar Market, where Khurana ji is going to meet them later, and not able to find any buses today; such a problem. She was growing anxious, still looking around, and Arjun decided to take charge. The rain had stopped again. He took the boy's hand in his own, and said, '*Chaliye*, I will get you something.' He waited for her to fold the umbrella, and then started walking, the boy between them, as they went around the roundabout and got onto the road leading towards Connaught Place, Arjun looking around for any taxi, and trying to make conversation with the boy. As they were crossing in front of Saint Columba School, he noticed a taxi coming out from the church inside, and he waved it down. '*Achcha* Bhabhi ji, I will take your leave now.' He stopped modestly to one side as they climbed in, and then waved at the boy. The taxi moved off, and he breathed deep, as he stood there on that tree-lined street, his good deeds of the day behind him now, hopefully. He lit a cigarette – he thought he deserved that, at least - and walked on towards Connaught place.

Next morning, Arjun scanned the papers for crime news, but did not find anything that could be connected to Billa and Ranga. He spent the day in his hotel room, resting and thinking about the life ahead of him. He had done his share of virtuous acts, he had even given up the love of his life. And for what? Misplaced ideas of promises and commitment and nobility? He was stuck in a time not of his own – he will not even be born for another decade! He had some money left, a small-time job as a teacher in the hills, and some precognition tools that he could use to make money when really required. Hopefully. Time to head back to *Agyatwaas*.

CHAPTER XIV

1978-2008

The Government Primary School near NalDamyanti Tal was stark in its beauty. The lake itself was about 400m away from the school. A natural body of water, neither too big to be incomprehensible, nor too small to be trivial. Tranquil clear water, fishes swimming boldly, trees and greenery all around, their reflections making the water appear green. There were hills all around, and mountains in the middle distance. The lake was one of the seven scattered in these hills – jointly called Sat Tal. Arjun found a house to live, about 20 minutes' walk to the school – in a village called Kuya-tal near Bhimtal. Basically a brick structure, single storied when he first took it, and which remained his home for more than 5 years. He grew a beard and came to be known as an eccentric to the people who would try to get close to him. After arriving from the year 2015 – 12 years ago now - life in the 60s & 70s itself had not been a cake-walk, but Lucknow was the capital city after all, the University still prestigious, and he had started getting used to "new" things like running water, toilet flush, cooking gas, appliances, motor transport, radio. Coming to Bhimtal was like experiencing another time-shift. There was no running water, no cooking gas, limited electricity, and not much furniture. He had to hire a servant to heat water and cook & clean for him, and he lived hermit-like – teaching and walking - except in one respect.

In Mahabharata, Prince Arjuna had spent *Agyatwaas* as a Eunuch, while this Arjun's experience was very different. It started as a distraction for him, and then it became a refuge from the questions emptiness kept throwing at him. Soon after his arrival at the school and the village, he had started receiving hints and solicitations – at his regular tea stall, in the market, shopping for groceries, and where he used to get his hair cut. 'Master Saheb lives alone, if he ever needs anything...", or, 'it is very cold today, should I send someone?" He understood the suggestions, and laughed them off, at first. But then, in the evenings, the vacant walls, the creeping darkness, started getting to him. The questions that had no answers only got louder in the silence – 'What would Nalini be doing right now? Why did I have to do this? What if she does not find happiness elsewhere? But oh, what if she does!?" One night, he found that he was talking loudly to himself, and decided he had to break out of this cycle. The "nobility" of his sacrifice (for what?) made it easier to throw away all his obligations like a worn-out shirt. He did not owe anybody anything, anymore. It was like starting with a really blank slate. Except that he was a postgraduate in history from Allahabad history, and a teacher by chance. Or was it by choice?

Anyway, next day, Arjun spoke to the tea-stall guy – Bahadur – and worked out a system in which to allow himself to be lost in the dance of pure bodily need. At least his own. No emotions were involved, no sleeping together or the anticipation of waking up together, or even of the feeling of fulfilment. The money he paid was not much, though just enough for him to feel exonerated after every transaction. He paid for the service provided, and that was it. Kept away the craziness, after all. He was angry with himself, the world, the situation he was in, and though he felt ashamed, whenever he looked in the mirror, it was an effective distraction.

Otherwise, he was an everyman, trying to make a living teaching children, and staying away from everything he had known since his arrival in this world in 1966. But, part of him still wanted to stay connected. After all, he had the urge to know what really happens to Rana and Nalini. If they got together, he could at least rest assured that he had finally fulfilled his original mission. He had no idea of what to do after that happened, of course, but he was not thinking that far.

In late-September 1979, he took leave for a week and caught the night train to Lucknow, in search of news. In his bearded and long-haired disguise, he was sure no one would recognize him – except Nalini, he felt sure – so he just had to be careful. Loitering around the Coffee House and the university campus – except the Economics building - he eavesdropped and probed. Something was definitely brewing, and Ranveer Singh was back in Lucknow now, living somewhere in Mahanagar. But Arjun did not get any concrete news, and so expanded his search. First, a quick walk through Paper Mill Colony, where the Shukla family was living. There was a park in front of their block of Flats, where they lived on the first floor. It was likely that Nalini was still living in the University housing, and he could not dare go there. All he got were glimpses of his mother-in-law – Chachi - on the terrace. Then, a trip to Gole Market near Mahanagar, which had recently started growing as a shopping area, and while walking around, Arjun ran into someone he had known – Ram Aasray! Yes, the first person he had met in this timeline some 13 years ago – who now had a sweet shop on the back side of Gole Market. Ram Aasray did not recognize him at first – after all, Arjun had changed – but then remembered (with visible pleasure) when prompted. Ram also looked different – better clothes, less servitude, and definitely more prosperous – and some of the old bonds strengthened over tea and samosas. Arjun told him some kind of sad-story about having to live away in a small town to take care of an old relative, but did not go into details. As luck would have it, the house that Rana had rented was a stone's throw from this sweet shop. Ram Aasray had known Ranveer Singh from before, of course, though, as he put it – 'he is a big saheb, how would he remember me?' Overall, the Lucknow trip gave Arjun a lot of food for thought, but nothing could have really satisfied him, anyway. And he went back to his mountains.

• • •

In January 1980, he got the news from his contact that Rana & Nalini were getting married, and he rushed to Lucknow. On the day of the wedding, evening found him sitting again in the same park in the middle of Paper Mill Colony, sitting and gazing up at the shamiana that had been erected on the terrace of Shukla ji's flat. Difficult to see anything, frustratingly, but he sat for more than hour in that cold dark evening, waiting, and hoping to catch a glimpse of someone he could recognize. There were children hanging around in the park, even at that late hour, and playing games of their own making. Thankfully, they largely stayed away from him. Getting up and pacing around, he noticed Mohan leave with his family, and felt an urge to shout out to him, to show himself; but it was only for a fleeting moment. Too late for giving in to such urges now! Finally, he saw a car pulling up, and then the main wedding party getting out of the flat, and five people squeezing into the Ambassador car. In the rush, he could only make out Nalini's parents and Rana, but could not see Nalini in the hubub. His eyes were watering, but he lit a beedi to occupy his hands. Then he was out of the park and walking in the wake of the car. No risk of anyone recognizing him now, he felt sure. Streetlights threw circles of dirty orange colour into the smog of the winter evening, and he felt like he was floating, watching the last of his moorings getting unhitched. He was free now, but was it heaviness he still felt in his heart? Cursing loudly, he threw away the beedi angrily, and walked faster. Finally, a rickshaw! He got into it, asking the man to take him to Gole Market.

He did not even try to meet Ram Aasray this time, but got down from the rickshaw, and loitered near a *paan* shop, muttering to himself, and cursing, again and again. Finally, he gathered himself and walked towards Rana's house – lighted up like it was Diwali! People going in and coming out, but no one he could recognize. Arjun was not sure what he was waiting for, but he could not be anywhere else at this time, anyway. So, he came back, and slid into the eatery that Ram Aasray ran. The owner was not around – it was almost 8PM on this cold winter night, and Arjun forced himself to eat two samosas and one plate of gajar ka halwa. The samosas were refried but the stuffing inside was tasty enough. And the halwa was delicious – hot, and just sweet enough. Celebrating his ex-wife's wedding – he thought and laughed aloud at his quirkiness, while Ram Aasray's son, who was manning the counter looked on warily at the bearded, be-shawled customer. Finally, a cup of tea, and then Arjun was outside in the cold again, lighting up a beedi and walking along the road towards Wireless. Still aimless, but strangely hesitant to leave. Just a few feet away from the *Chauraha*, there was a rickshaw standing to one side, with the puller sitting nearby at a makeshift bonfire – now almost gone – and smoking a beedi. Arjun stopped and crouched down next to the dwindling fire, thankful for the heat, and just said "*ram-ram*" to the rickshaw-puller. He got up in a few seconds, and paced around, when his eyes fell on two men standing at the *paan* shop he had left a few minutes ago. He could recognize Mohan and Rana even from that distance, and gazed at the figures, his mind blank now. He was not going to see Nalini today – he told himself. Perhaps never. Abruptly, he dragged his eyes away, and got into the rickshaw. 'Let us go', he said, and then, they left.

After that he went back to Bhimtal, and drowned himself into work and the routine of daily life. He would later think of this as his most aimless period and it lasted about three years. It was as if he had no moorings left, no one to cherish, nothing to really look forward to. Except there were. He had the school, the children, and the mountains and the lakes. And somewhat strangely, sometimes it felt enough. The earth kept rotating, seasons kept changing, and his concerns, his losses seemed petty compared to the reality of the world.

• • •

In 1981, he came to know about the birth of a daughter in the Rana family. The final nail in the coffin of his self-aborted love-life, he thought, and pushed away the idea of going to Lucknow. What did he have to do with her any more, anyway?

In 1984, when Arjun's official age was 42, he came to know about a new missionary school opening in the area. He applied, and moved there as a senior Teacher, and found the new school a different experience, and his knowledge of English much more useful. The students were also from richer families, children of new professionals and businessmen sending their kids for a boarding school experience. He got a house at the under-construction campus, and got very busy setting up the curriculum and school infrastructure.

While he was busy thus, Operation Blue Star happened in nearby Punjab, and soon, as he already knew, the Prime minister was going to be assassinated – on 31 October. So he tried again, sending an anonymous letter to the New Delhi Police, about the PM's body-guards, and how they could try to kill her. But there was no visible effect of that, and that evening, he heard the announcement on the radio. And then the news about the riots, and targeted killings of sikh families – in Delhi, and at various locations in north Indian states. There were not that many Sikhs around where he lived, and the local impact was minimal.

Next year, he bought 4 acres of land in Bhimtal, and started thinking of settling down. But he could not really focus on learning farming or tourism or any new form of business. Teaching had become his core field of interest and experience, after almost 2 decades in it, and he could not deny it, nor move completely away from it. So, he continued his dual life: a teacher in the hills, and a wanderer in the plains.

All this time, Arjun had also been secretly worried about an important milestone which was approaching inexorably - his upcoming birth in Allahabad sometime before July 1988! Firstly, he did not know his exact date of birth, only the official one – 15 July. Secondly, he did not know his real parents, and the official entry about his birth hospital. What if he did nothing about it? Would it mean another Arjun would be born, who would be finally adopted by the Saxena couple? And if he really had to somehow influence his conception, then he had to start nine months earlier – in October of 1987. But he had no clue where, and it was too late for that now, anyway.

• • •

Arjun travelled to Allahabad on the last Sunday of June 1988. He checked into a small hotel, just across the Old Naini bridge, close to the Grand Trunk Road. That evening, when he felt that the summer day had lost some of its heat, he started out from his hotel in Civil Lines, and took a rickshaw to GTB Nagar, near Habib Park. C-755, GTB Nagar, Kareli, that was their address for the first decade of his life. In that time! Now, he was almost half-century old, heading back to his childhood home, where he would be about to be born again. Maybe.

As the rickshaw turned into the C-Block road, nothing looked familiar. The last time he was here was in October 2015, in what seemed a previous life now. He was 27 then, and was getting over a heart-break. But this place was much older. His memories of childhood had become very hazy with age, but at some level, it also felt safer to think that this was all unfamiliar.

While looking at the house numbers, he noticed that they were next to Habib Park now. There was a hedge around it (wasn't there a wall here later?), so he could make out the flagpole in the middle of the park. That triggered some memory somewhere, but he did not delve deeper into it. Arjun noticed house number 750 and brought his attention back. He asked the rickshaw to stop under the shade of a tree, and got down, telling the man to wait. The road was tarred, and heat was still rising from it after the hot summer day. 751, 752, and he walked on slowly, till 755 approached, the iron gate sending messages to his overworked brain. There was a guava tree inside the wall, with branches growing till outside. Arjun stopped at the gate, and considered his next move. What if he found his adaptive parents here? He thought, and looked around. The rickshaw was stopped a little distance behind, under the shade. He pushed at the gate and saw the flowering plant just inside, and the name "*Kaner*" popped into his head. Bright yellow colour and texture was again cajoling his memory banks, but he looked around, and there were potted plants, a couple of garden chairs sitting by themselves, and then the brown painted door with metal mesh on it – leading inside his "home". He felt giddy and stopped to take a deep breath. There was a smell of cooking from inside, the biting tinge of Asafoetida, and it made him disoriented. There was nothing like this in his childhood memories, however dim they were. But there was a more recent memory of Asafoetida – Nalini used to cook with it! Arjun shook his head, and moving towards the door, knocked on the wooden portion with his knuckles.

A middle-aged woman came to the door, and looked at him through the net. 'Who is it', she asked in Hindi, suspicion in her tone. Arjun folded his hands, and tried in a mild voice, 'Does Saxena saheb live here?' The outside light was turned on (it was getting darker), and the woman continued from behind the door. 'There is no Saxena here, bhaisab,' she must have gauged his age as similar to hers. It was only then that Arjun noticed the nameplate below the lightbulb – "S.C. Mishra". She continued, when Arjun stayed quiet and only expressed surprise through his expression, 'what address was given to you?' And Arjun, fumbling, 'address was this only - 755, near Habib Park. The women, helpful now, 'it could be A-block, on the other side of the park. This is C –block. And we are living here for more than 4 years.' She added, unnecessarily. 'Ok, *behenji*, thank you,' he folded his palms again, and turned around to leave.

'You will have some water to drink?' She was softening now. But Arjun had no time for that, and departed politely, closing the gate behind him. As he approached the rickshaw under the tree, his mind went through the possibilities. Either,

(1) Arjun2 is born, but is not adopted by his parents, so he will grow up as orphan, or somebody else's adopted son, or

(2) Arjun2 is born, is adopted by the same people, but they are living somewhere else, so he will grow more or less as before, or

(3) Arjun2 is not born, so he is out of the equation completely.

Sitting in the rickshaw, Arjun asked to be taken back to his hotel, and started ticking off – ideal case (for ease of mind) is Option 3, of course, and he has no way of confirming the possibility of options 1 and 2 till at least two decades later. Arjun gave up the search at this point, and told himself not to worry about his re-birth, at least till the new millennium.

• • •

By the end of 1990, he had shifted to Delhi, opened a small tuition center, and started studying the stock market seriously. He rented a house on Hanuman Road, near Cannaught Place, and also bought a colour TV, so that he could watch a news program he had started liking - "The World this Week" by Prannoy Roy. He had a decent bank balance, properties and other assets by then. And he had the advantage (however diluted by now) of knowing the future. A future he had already lived in before.

In May 1991, Arjun knew that Rajiv Gandhi was going to be killed by a terrorist suicide-bomber, but again felt helpless in changing anything. Like he had done for Indira Gandhi, he wrote anonymous letters and sent to the Delhi and Coimbatore, giving them a date for the targeted assassination. But it did not seem to have any effect on the events of the day, and people died.

In July, he visited Lucknow again - watching from a distance as the grih-pravesh for Rana's new house in Indira Nagar was being celebrated. Besides Rana, he observed Nalini, Mohan, and the children – Ranjini and Ravi. Being at a safe distance, he could not make out the features very clearly, but the daughter was too young. Seeing Nalini after all these years was painful, and from the distance, he tried to find some change in her, but failed, his eyes burning. On the way back from his vigil, he stopped for lunch at a Dosa place, where they were playing a song from the new Hindi film – '*dil hai ki manta nahin...* (the heart does not listen...)'

Towards the end of next year, he watched the Babri Masjid demolition live on TV, and wondered at the vanity of human beings, about believers staking claim to saving gods and their birthplaces.

In 1993, he sold his Bhimtal land bought 8 years ago, at almost 3X the original rate. Knowing the future (however vaguely), he bought 100 shares during the Infosys IPO that year, and also invested large sums in Wipro shares.

In 1996, he applied for and got a landline internet connection from BSNL. Three decades after he had bought an iPhone (in his previous life!) This was a dial-up connection, with speeds as slow as a snail, but Arjun had basically forgotten his earlier times by now, and it seemed ok for the time being. He was learning and experiencing everything anew, it appeared to him.

In 1997, he was again in Lucknow in September, and met Ramesh, who was working at Rana's house since July of that year. This meeting happened at Bhootnath market, where Ramesh had gone to buy groceries. Arjun introduced himself as an old friend of Rana from Calcutta, paid him some money, ostensibly to take better care of Rana and his family, but also asked him to keep this a secret. This was a gamble – to have an inside source for future. And even if Ramesh divulges anything to Rana, Arjun was confident they will not be able to connect this stranger (from Calcutta) with the past. Arjun ensured sending some money to Ramesh after this on a regular basis.

Next year in March, continuing to exploit his precognition powers, he betted on Prime Minister Vajpayee winning the confidence vote by 13 votes, and won big - in a *satta* market being run in Sadar Bazar.

In 2000, Arjun bought his first mobile phone (again after 33 years) – a basic Nokia handset for making calls and sending messages, using the alarm, and sometimes the flashlight. During a visit to Lucknow, he met Ramesh, and got to know from him that Ranjini was going to Allahabad for studying Engineering.

In 2004, Arjun made a killing again in the local betting market, by staking a substantial amount on Congress forming the new national government. All the opinion polls were predicting a narrow win for the BJP and allies, but Arjun knew that Manmohan Singh would be Prime Minster for the next ten years! The same year, Ramesh also left the Rana household, and started learning heavy-equipment maintenance and driving. Arjun continued to fund Ramesh, believing that he would continue to be a link and a source of information.

In 2006, at one of the first Conferences on Technology in Education, Arjun met Neel Kotwal. The boy was working at Infosys, had an interest in online education and training, and even at the first meeting, shone as a bright mind. When Arjun asked him about his parents, Neel told him that his father had died in 1978, when the Air India 855 Bombay-Dubai flight crashed during take-off. In fact, Neel was not yet born when that happened, so he never saw his father. Arjun immediately identified with this – not having seen his own father ever – only the adopted one. While expressing his condolences, Arjun also relived that new year's day of 1978, in Bombay, when he had been running around Dadar, trying to find a phone to talk to the airport authorities. And one victim of that failure of his, was in front of him now. He excused himself, and wandered off, not able to talk normally for some time. Later, he ran into Neel again, and during their discussion, Neel mentioned to Arjun about Khan Academy – a new venture started in the US that year only, which provided online classes in the form of short videos. They talked about this for some time, and Arjun was impressed by the understanding, clarity and sincerity of the young man. They exchanged contact details, and their conversation led Arjun to finally decide to invest in this interesting new field. Next year, he registered a new company in the EduTech area, with some confidence in growing it further in the future.

Over the years, in this new timeline that he had created, Arjun came to terms with this experience of reliving a life since 1988. From when he was originally (?) born on the Earth, and spent 27 years of his life (however mundane or joyless), before deciding to enter that portal and break through the fabric of time. And what he had already realized was that the gift of precognition worked in such a way that large, earth-shaking events were difficult, or even impossible, to change. He already knew the next big terrorist attack (In Mumbai, December 2008), but could not figure out a way of stopping it. There was an inexorable machinery, with connecting threads, which lead to such events, and no intervention was possible, except by making a really big scene about it. And he was not ready to do that, and open himself up to enquiries and investigations. Yes, you could influence more immediate or intimate events (accidents like that of Mohan's death, or one-off crimes like the kidnapping and murder of the Chopra siblings), but otherwise, you could only exploit upcoming events in your favor – like killing yourself in a train accident, or making money in betting on a known-but-unexpected-outcome. So, Arjun consoled himself, and focused on doing what he liked, and thought he was good at. And he had started with clear advantages in this life, so he continued to...

CHAPTER XV

2008-2016

On that evening of July 2008, he got a phone call from Ramesh in Lucknow. News about the worsening health of "Mem sab", and that she might not survive for long. And he compressed the dread of the last few days into a single-minded focus on travelling. If somehow, his presence in Lucknow helped her, great, otherwise.... His thoughts paused there. Otherwise? He had to end his life, of course. What was he doing here anyway?

That evening, before leaving with a small bag for the station, he handed a file of documents to Mahinder, his driver/cook/friend of many years. 'Just in case, something happens, remember who you have to give it to?' It was less of a question than a statement, and Mahinder only folded his hands, mumbling agreement at him.

Arjun took a taxi, and after a short drive, managed to catch the Lucknow mail from New Delhi Railway station – Sleeper class, since there was no berth available in AC. After he had settled down and the train had started out, he went through a check-list. His going-away checklist. He had last made such a list before leaving Lucknow for Ahmedabad that day in August 1977. And that kiss was still there in his memory, if only as a splinter in the skin now. And before that, that Holi day on 1967 (was it?) when he had decided that his time-travel assignment was over, and he could go back to his time – having saved Mohan from death, somehow. And the panic he had almost drowned in, when he had started imagining the consequences. Hypothetical consequences, but with enough severity to stop him from trying to travel back (forward to 2015). Was it fear, or anticipation though? By now, as the train cluttered on the tracks, Arjun can recall very few memories of his original time-line. Where he was adopted as a baby, and brought up in the Saxena family in Allahabad.

As the train pulled into Ghaziabad, Arjun settled back in the window seat, and squeezed his forehead above his eyes. He had first grown up as Arjun Saxena, became an adult, and then travelled half-a-century back to re-live his life. How old was he now? He tried to calculate and failed beyond a general "late-sixties" age-marker. He was getting old, and perhaps it is just as well. But Nalini.....? His thoughts failed him.

As the new day started, he got up groggy from a nightmare, as the train crawled and then stopped somewhere near Alamnagar. He folded his long sheet – *Khays* - with slow, measured movements, and then went to wash his face and ease his bladder. His knees felt okay, better than they generally felt in colder weather, and after washing and drying his face, he sat down and tried not to think about... her! After a few more agonizing stops and starts, the train entered the long platform at Lucknow. Arjun walked out of the station with his bag on one shoulder, and hired an auto to the hospital. The hospital Ramesh had mentioned in Indira Nagar.

It was still early enough that there was no crowd one would normally expect to see at a hospital. Fortunately, there was a tea stall open nearby, and Arjun went in and found a stool to sit. He asked for tea and ate a couple of rusks with it. He felt strong enough after this to go inside and enquire. The day was already growing warm, and the receptionist was checking in for her duty hours. He asked for Cardiology ICU, and was directed to the second floor. Arjun looked around for a lift, and went up in the rickety affair. At his destination, as he opened the grille and stepped out, he was thinking, 'now what?' He had come this far on autopilot, but how was he to find more? His steps slowed down, as he shifted the bag to his other shoulder, and followed the arrows to Cardiology. There was no one around, but as he hesitated in front of the door, it opened and three people walked out – two doctors, and a young girl who was rummaging in her purse. Arjun stepped to one side, as they passed him by, and saw that the girl had taken out a mobile phone. The doctors went into another door, and she walked off towards the stairs and started climbing down. Arjun heard her say "Papa?" in a voice just barely controlled. That was Nalini's daughter, he realized. But, he turned around again and pushed open the ICU door this time, walking in without another thought. There was a male nurse standing at a table just inside, making some notes in a files, and looked up questioningly at the old man. 'Just one minute, beta,' Arjun spoke without letting his voice tremble, and, 'only want to see...', and with that non-threatening but urgent statement, he was inside. There were four beds there, with only two occupied, and there she was on the last bed against the wall. Nalini. White hair, eyes closed (thankfully), hospital dress, tubes, wires, but the face was familiar and looked unlined, as beautiful as he remembered. At peace. The nurse was at his shoulder now, and Arjun turned around with an effort, 'no, he is not here. Must be some mistake...', and he left the ICU, the floor, the hospital. Then he was on the road again. Wondering what to do now.

A rickshaw was dropping someone near the hospital gate, and Arjun moved towards him, to ask him for a hotel nearby. The rickshawala was helpful, and offered to take 'baba' there – Hotel Green View – only a few minutes away. There was nothing else to do for him but wait, and better to do it in a hotel room. There was a single "deluxe" room available, and paying the one-day advance, Arjun checked in.

He woke up with a start and fumbled to look at the time – it was 11:30 already. After the uneasy sleep in the train the previous night, he had thought of resting for some time, and had fallen asleep on the hotel bed. Except for the whirring of the fan, it was very quiet in the room, and Arjun felt a strange sense of closure; as if everything was ending today. Perhaps it would be his last day as well. Along with the bad taste in his mouth, he could feel the dread of Nalini's death on his mind. How do you go on after that?

It was after a couple of hours before he reached the hospital again. After he had taken bath, changed, eaten some light lunch. No harm in doing the usual mundane things. Important to keep the perspective. At the hospital, as he came out on the 2nd floor, the first person he saw was Madhavi – Nalini's sister! She had changed a lot – and who hadn't really – but he could recognize her. She was talking to a doctor just outside Cardiology, and Arjun remembered that she must be a doctor herself now. He turned sideways, but waited, pretending to make a call from his mobile phone. "Let me see," he heard his ex-sister-in-law say, and then she went inside the ICU. The doctor walked away, and Arjun was left waiting again. He had not kept track of Dr. Madhavi's whereabouts, but it was really heartening to see her here. He tried to remember when he had last seen her, and could only manage a vague memory of Diwali (was it in 1976?) sweets and the two sisters chatting together and laughing at something, and of feeling awkward in their presence, as if being laughed at himself. In the hospital corridor, leaning against the wall, the memory brought out a weak smile, and he wondered about life. Then suddenly, there was a rush of people coming up the steps, and he froze. A young boy, by the side of Ranjini, turned the corner and approached the ICU door. Confused now, and scared, he turned around and started walking the other way. The ICU door opened and closed behind him, and after a few feet, he swiveled his head around once and saw Rana coming out of the lift, helped by Ramesh. Oh, so even Ramesh had come! Like vultures gathering – his first bitter thought was – and he cursed himself. Rana appeared old, with a stumbling walk and sagging shoulders. Arjun watched him with sympathy – there is no escape from loss, is there? In another timeline, Colonel Rana persuaded his tenant – Arjun - to change the past to reunite with Nalini, and all of that happened, but not as planned. And now this? What was the point of it all? Where does the "love" go when you lose your loved ones, he wondered, and went downstairs to wait at the hospital reception.

He was checking his watch when Ranjini came down the stairs – it was after 2PM. She was red-faced and had tear-streaks below her eyes, and Arjun knew. Even before he heard her speak on the phone – "Yes Uncle, ma is..., no more. Please come, Papa needs help." Arjun bent his head down and cried without a sound. When he lifted his head to look up again, the same boy was holding Ranjini's shoulders and they stood quietly, Ranjini's eyes wild and hopeless. Arjun thought of getting up, but found he did not have the strength to do that. The boy was respectful but firm, as he kept talking to his "didi" and mumbling words of courage – that is how it appeared to Arjun. He must be Madhavi's son.

The two cousins went back upstairs, and Arjun bent his head down again. Time for him to go as well. Nalini was no more, except perhaps in memories. People say that you can keep dead people in your heart, but Arjun could not feel any such presence. But then he remembered that he had so far kept a living presence in his heart, but now? He walked outside, and stopped near a rickshaw. "Where to, *chacha*?" For a few moments, Arjun could not remember the name of the hotel he had checked into, and fumbled, 'there is a hotel, nearby, green-colored walls...," and it came, 'Green View!' He climbed onto the seat with some effort, and sat back, as the rickshaw took him away from a dead ex-wife. The love of his life, gone from the Earth. Forever.

In the hotel room, he lay down on the bed, wondering how the breath continues, even when you are feeling like a sock wrung-out to dry. He felt his heart with his palm, and marveled at the beats he could actually time. But really, there was no other way now! He will give up his life, and take his secrets with him. There is nothing else left to be done. The brightness that had kept him here, in this timeline, had become blinding now. He could not bear it any longer.

He must have dozed off again, because when he woke up, the sun had gone down towards the horizon. For a short period after waking up, he imagined he had dreamt everything, but then, looking at the hotel walls, the reality struck him hard and he cried.

That evening, at the banks of Gomti river, close to Nalini's pyre, as he stood preparing himself to end his life by jumping into the dark waters, he was stopped by Ranjini. He spoke to Nalini's daughter, and an idea germinated in his mind, which also gave him some kind of a reason for living. As the days passed, he found he could continue to breath.

Breath, and work.

• • •

As the stock market tumbled, Arjun was unperturbed. He had, after all, already made his divestments at the right time, and saved some for his new venture. In early 2009, while the Right to Education Act was being discussed in the Indian Parliament, Arjun formulated a plan for the launch of a start-up, with a seed funding of 50 L. The overarching idea was universalization of education, with a focus on online learning, on the backbone of app development. He invited Neel Kotwal, having already met him before at a conference, as well as Nalini's daughter, to Delhi. Arjun introduced them to each other, and to some other members of his team. After the announcements were made, Arjun took them aside, and offered them jobs – Neel as marketing head, and Ranjini as Technology/ Development head. He also asked them to name their packages. The start-up would be called "Vidya Technologies".

• • •

When Ranjini and Neel got married in May 2010, Arjun made sure he was not there for the court registration, or for the dinner reception in Lucknow. He stayed back in Delhi (on purpose), and only blessed them over a phone call. He knew that if he came face-to-face with Rana, there was no way to stay incognito, and felt it was still not the right time to come out of his *Agyatwaas*.

The company grew, with the young couple moving between Delhi and Lucknow, and enjoying the work and their life together. "Vidya" launched its first online education portal in the middle of 2012, and things got very busy for everyone associated with the company.

By the end of that year though, Arjun had to struggle with a big decision: Whether to intervene in the horrific crime about to be committed? This was the second big & immediate "bad thing", he had been preparing himself to face since the time he had accepted that he was going to live on in this timeline of the world.

In his earlier lifetime, he had a serious attack of moral panic when this crime had been commited in the winter of 2012. He was 24, in his first job at Dehradun, with a mostly protected childhood, except for some rebellious friends in Roorkee. Money was never a problem, but he had managed to stay away from most college-life "sins". So, when that "gang-rape" and "murder" happened in Delhi, his first reaction was disgust, but also an increase in self-awareness. What would he have done in those situations? "The problem is us", as he was coming to accept. Some of those memories were now gone, but he had read and re-read his notes from Wikipedia over the years, and tried to retain the main components of the man-made tragedy.

This is what he remembered: a young man and a woman, after watching a movie at the Saket PVR, were going to board a private bus on the evening of 16 December, and going to be brutally assaulted by six people, and left to die on the roadside. The girl, with severe internal injuries will die after a few days, even after extraordinary medical efforts. The criminals were going to be caught and given the death sentence. The case was going to be highly publicized in India and even globally, and would lead to legal advancements in rape, assault and murder cases, and perhaps also to increased introspection and sensitivity.

The question was, is it better to save the victims from their ordeal (and painful death, in the case of the girl)? Or to let the events unfold, so that the laws become stricter, and (hopefully) act as deterrent for future crimes? How to weigh the two side-by-side? On one side was an immediate act of inhuman brutality, and the opportunity to save the victims. On the other, a future anticipation of stricter laws and improved social situation. Finally, he decided to worry about the here-and-now, and let the future look after itself. There will be other crimes and the resulting outrage and response, he reasoned. Human beings have a tendency to surprise society by showing what they were capable of, in terms of extraordinary brutality, and going beyond the then prevalent moral compass. Things changed, but people could always be relied upon to reach new depths of transgression.

But he was in his 70s now, and needed help, he admitted to himself. Neel and Ranjini were the first two names that came to mind, but Arjun was not sure what kind of story he will have to make. After a light lunch, while soaking in the afternoon sun from his apartment balcony, he formed a plan.

On the morning of 16 December, a Sunday, Arjun called Neel and Ranjini, and asked to take Ranjini out for some time that evening.

With Mahinder at the wheel of his Innova, Arjun picked up Ranjini from their Gurgaon apartment in Sector 24, near the Delhi border. Below Galaxy Apartments, Neel was waiting with Ranjini in the gathering dusk of the winter evening. Neel tried to ask jokingly, 'at least tell me where you are taking her.' Arjun fended him off with, 'mostly driving and talking; you focus on the cooking today.' Ranjini hugged Neel and got in, a broad smile on her face. As they moved out, she looked back, waved, and made a face, 'poor guy.' Arjun laughed heartily, and started talking about Vidya, to keep her mind off the job in front of them, or the explanation of it. Mahinder already knew the route, and caught Tulsi Marg near Le Meridian hotel, moving fast towards Mehrauli and Saket. In about 30 min, when they could see Qutub Minar on their left, Ranjini changed the conversation. She started out by saying that they haven't seen even Qutub Minar yet! 'We have to find time to come here.' Arjun nodded, and agreed. 'Working too hard?' He added, and Ranjini was thoughtful for a moment, before, 'of course. And you know that very well. But still, we don't work on Sundays, and even then, somehow, there are other things to do. And I also try to visit Papa, back in Lucknow frequently, so, you know.' She stopped, but before Arjun could start something else, she turned around on her seat towards him, and directed her eyes at his face, curiosity and excitement in them, 'when are you going to tell me about today's program?' As the car turned right towards Badarpur, Arjun explained, briefly, 'not much. We will go to PVR Saket. They have nice coffee there, and lots of good stuff to eat. I have to meet someone there, and then we will go to Dwarka for some of my special weekly shopping. That's it, I will drop you back before 10PM.'

Ranjini was making a face, again. 'Really! That's it? I had no idea you liked traveling around so much. RG uncle, you are one weird person, if you don't mind me saying!' She knew she could get away with that, with him for sure. They turned left towards Saket, and Arjun stayed quiet, looking at the time on his phone. In another couple of minutes, they could see the PVR building on their right. Arjun asked Mahinder to drop them on the Community center road, and then turn around and bring the car at the same stop. Then, with Ranjini's help, he crossed the street, and then walked over the paved area to the PVR building. Around the entrance, there were food stalls, well-lighted, with mostly-young people already thronging the area. But it was not overly crowded, and Arjun lead Ranjini to a café that provided a side-view of the PVR entrance. It was cold, but under the lights and near the cooking areas, it felt fine. Even for Arjun, who could bear cold weather less and less. Once they ordered (Coffee for Arjun, and Coffee and blueberry muffin for Ranjini), they sat down, and now he explained to her further. In a few minutes, he will point out a couple coming out of the theater and Ranjini has to go and talk to them. Arjun told their names, and only said that he knows the girl's father very well. Ranjini had questions, but kept them to herself for now. Another few minutes passed, and Arjun appeared concerned, but finished his coffee, and asked for another. 'It is cold!' Ranjini grimaced and finishing her muffin, asked him, 'I will make a quick phone call to Neel, see what's he doing?' But Arjun was suddenly alert, staring at the entrance, where a couple was now coming out, smiling together at something. He pointed them out to Ranjini, 'the girl in the white jacket, and the boy with her!' Ranjini got up and started moving towards them. The girl was much younger than her, plain-looking, but confident in herself. In front now, Ranjini lifted her hand and said the name of the girl, who stopped and asked her, respectfully, 'yes, ma'am?' Ranjini quickly introduced herself, and continued in English - that they would not know her, but her "Uncle" (she turned out and pointed at Arjun), wanted to talk to them. The boy was unsure, asking, 'but who is he?' Ranjini only said what she knew, addressing the girl, 'he knows your father very well.' She started moving back after saying this, and felt sure the couple would follow behind her. There was nothing to fear, at this stage. They crossed over to the café seating, and Arjun got up, and raised his hand in a blessing. He addressed the girl in Hindi, 'I am Sharma uncle, and know your father very well. He has, uh,.. worked for me in the past. Sit, sit.' He was trying to nudge them to trust him, and tried to keep it casual. He continued in English, 'How was the movie? Ranjini, have you seen "Life of Pi" yet?' They were sitting down, the boy still unsure and wary, but the girl appeared to be comfortable in their company. Ranjini had started praising the movie, and the girl agreed with her wholeheartedly, speaking in a mix of English and Hindi. Arjun intervened again, speaking forcefully in English, as if the matter was already settled, 'OK, so we are going towards Dwarka, and you two can come with us. Getting a bus or auto will not be easy now.' His last sentence tilted it for them, and then they were walking back together, Arjun with the girl in the front, asking about her work (she was a physiotherapist), and Ranjini behind them, with the boy, looking slightly unhappy but resigned to the situation.

Mahinder opened the doors, and Arjun got into the front seat, asking the youngsters to get comfortable in the back. The girl sat in the middle, between Ranjini and her boyfriend, and the second-row seat was big enough in an Innova anyway. The first thing Arjun asked, after they had started out, 'you still live in Dwarka Sector 4, right? I have to go to Sector 3, and can drop you nearby.' And the girl, 'no sir, in Sector 13, and it is just near to Sector 3'. Arjun nodded, and looking around, asked Mahinder, 'very difficult to get autos from here?' And Mahinder, perhaps already coached, 'no sir, Sunday evening, they are all drinking at the local *theka*!' He spoke in a dry monotone, and after a pause, Ranjini laughed out, and the couple smiled in agreement. Then Ranjini's phone rang, and she spoke to Neel in English, 'yes, yes, all right. Going to Dwarka with uncle, and be back home soon. No, don't worry, I ate a large muffin...' Their conversation went on, while the young couple next to her conversed in undertones. Arjun was looking around, and stiffened when he saw a white private bus stopped ahead, seeking passengers. Ranjini noticed him turning around to watch, and wondered.

In about 45 minutes, they entered Dwarka, after passing Hauz Khas, Munirka, around the airport, and then through Palam. Arjun spoke to Mahinder again, and then asked the girl, 'You will be able to go from Sector 13 bus stop?' When she nodded vigorously, Arjun turned towards the boy, 'please be with her till she reaches home.' He had spoken so directly, and in a tone mixing request with direction, in the right amounts, that the boy could not disagree. The girl spoke up again, as they turned right on Central Road, 'but please uncle, you should come home.' And Arjun, thanking her, 'tell Badri I will meet him some other time.'

They got down near the bus stop, and the girl, after thanking Ranjini first, folded her hands at Arjun, and thanked him again. The boy also bobbed his head, mumbling something, and then they were walking down the street leading inside the Sector. Arjun got out too, and joined Ranjini in the back.

As they turned around, the first thing Ranjini asked him was about his "work" in Sector 3. Arjun looked at her blankly, and then, remembering, 'oh, yes. I had thought of buying some frozen meat there, but, it may be too late now for that!' Ranjini tried again, and asked him to tell her more about what happened today. Arjun just shook his head, 'even if I told it, you may not understand.' Ranjini showed some annoyance then, saying that he can trust her with a company, but not with something like this, and then became silent. Not sullen, because that was not in her nature.

Finally, just before reaching Gurgaon, Arjun seemed to relent, and said that he will explain, but that she should keep it with herself. Then he corrected himself, allowing Neel to be told, but no one else. He lied, about the object, but not wholly about the subject, 'she is the daughter of someone I loved a lot, but could not be together with. That's all. I got to know that the girl was in Saket today, and thought I would give her a lift. And get to spend some time in her company. Do you understand?' And Ranjini was amazed, 'you are really something, RG uncle!! Hidden depths, wow!' Then she gave his shoulder a squeeze. She kept trying after that, but Arjun stubbornly refused to divulge any more. She was shaking her head (expressing amazed disbelief) when she got down, and said good night to him. 'Bye'.

Later that night, when she related the story to Neel, he also expressed admiration and surprise at the old man's secrets. He also pointed out that, given the age of the girl, RG would have been at least 50 when he met that lady! 'He has never married, right?' Ranjini had no answer.

• • •

Days, month, and almost three years passed, with Arjun getting older, and the couple working for him, growing in capability and independence. Narendra Modi became PM of the country, by a huge majority. Markets were booming, there were other Ed-Tech companies coming up now, and Arjun realized that the time would soon come when Neel and Ranjini would be in high market-demand. He worked with them in developing a subsidiary – VidyaLAYA – for solving basic concepts in different subjects – both sciences and social studies - and initially not with any specific exam or test in mind. But slowly it grew into an online last-minute preparatory center for some very specialized, niche exams and certifications. The parent company, Vidya turned profitable 4 years after starting. They sold majority stakes in VidyaLAYA in 2013, and made a lot of money. Time for an IPO, maybe, but he did not have the energy left in him to drive that effort. And finally, it depended on his team. He felt amazed that at one time, he had agreed to time-travel for the promise of 1.5 Crores only!

Arjun also had other things on his mind. In November 2015, without Ranjini's knowledge, he decided to visit the time portal site in Chand Bagh, on the 49th Anniversary of his arrival through that portal. On the afternoon of 26th November, a Thursday (again, after 49 years!), he stood at the IT College junction, and tried to remember that day, when he had left his original life (and time), with some papers, money, a few clothes, and went through the time portal for the last time. He had lived another full life since then, with the sheen of a time-traveller over him. He knew all the major things that were going to happen! And so the landmark in his mind was this: from now on, he was just a regular person. His time-traveling advantages disappeared from today. He had no idea what would happen tomorrow, who wins the next world cup, or becomes the next Prime Minister, or what tragedy will strike, in the form of an accident or earthquake or floods. From tomorrow, when he reads the newspaper, he will be able to feel surprise. Like normal people.

He also noticed signs of upcoming activity related to the Lucknow Metro construction. The route would cross IT college, and this could have an effect on the adjoining area, including Chand Bagh.

• • •

In March 2016, Arjun came to know of the Chand Bagh excavations being planned. It was not because of the Lucknow Metro though, but because the College management had decided to build a new building in that garden. The day before the planned excavation, Arjun went to Lucknow again. He left his tattered diary, packed in a polythene bag, at the Chand Bagh site, and made sure Ramesh found it. Then Arjun checked into a new hotel in Hazratganj. Two days later, he went to Rana's house to meet him. Their first meeting in 47 years!

• • •

Arjun's final confession:

"The only questions that remains to be answered is - why did I stay on in the past, after completing my job? The "Past" was truly like a foreign country, but I had my reasons.

Firstly, I fell in love with Nalini. No secrets there. And who would have not? I mean, everyone around her was that way. You know that very well!

Second, when it dawned on me - and you knew this as well - that returning through that hell's gate causes a reset in that timeline. So, going back would have been like jumping into a dark well, blindfolded. I could not even imagine what I would hit.

So I stayed. And slowly learned that I had managed to confound myself - between the apparent reason, and true purpose of my time-travel. The former being "saving Mohan's life", and the latter, of course – "Ranveer weds Nalini"! Now you see why I pretended my death? Because I realized I had to focus on the true purpose, and somehow, take myself out of the equation. Between you and Nalini.

Hmmm, how did I manage to live? It was finally, not very difficult, after a longish period of painful torture and questioning, and the *Agyatwaas*. Also because I had given birth to this timeline – this thread of life – and I had to witness how it unfolded. I could not miss that just because I had given up on my happiness.

Of course, since last-year November, my sheen is completely gone, and I'm a regular fellow. Not a time-traveller any more. That wall is now destroyed, anyway, and hopefully the time-portal with it.

I have understood one thing very clearly, if nothing else: there is no way to compare one timeline with another on any meaningful scale – ethical, economic or emotional. And no reason for regrets. Because scales measure endings, not the journey. And journeys are where life resides."

Afterward

Towards the end of March 2016, Ranjini and Neel are in Lucknow for the really-long-weekend (from Holi to Easter), and to their surprise, RG visits them on Saturday evening. Another surprise for Ranjini is that her father and RG have already met, probably in the last few days only, and seem to be on easy terms. Which is a relief, because she had sensed some misgiving, perhaps even jealousy, from her father towards her boss. So she had actually been anticipating some tussle between the two whenever they would meet.

Then she gives them a surprise of her own: the news of her pregnancy. And feels overwhelmed at the showering of congratulations and blessings by the two old men. Nalini's absence hangs over them, of course, but Ranjini is thankful for what she has. She will never know that RG was once married to her mother. Arjun has already convinced Rana on this point.

www.ingramcontent.com/pod-product-compliance
Lightning Source LLC
LaVergne TN
LVHW091304150826
845673LV00006B/1537

* 9 7 9 8 8 9 1 8 6 7 1 7 8 *